Pauline King

Alida Craig

Pauline King

Alida Craig

ISBN/EAN: 9783744679084

Printed in Europe, USA, Canada, Australia, Japan

Cover: Foto ©Raphael Reischuk / pixelio.de

More available books at **www.hansebooks.com**

ALIDA CRAIG

BY

PAULINE KING

WITH ILLUSTRATIONS BY

T. K. HANNA, Jr.

NEW-YORK
GEORGE H. RICHMOND & CO.
1896

ALIDA CRAIG

CHAPTER I

Mr. and Mrs. Beckington's house in Fiftieth Street just off Fifth Avenue is one of those landmarks of perfect good taste in the remodelling of the erstwhile brownstone front that have so changed, in the last few years, the dreary character of our city streets. The interior, too, has seemed to strike the happy medium between conventional ugliness and the prim arrangements of the artistic decorator, to which, while they may be pioneers of sweetness and light, it is often so difficult to apply the word home.

The Beckingtons' house was essentially a home. When Clarence Beckington's engagement was announced a few years ago, every one was astonished to find that his choice had hit upon a soft little dark-eyed beauty in her first season, and there was much shaking of heads, and direful prognostication that such a well-known clubman would need a good deal stronger pair of hands, to make him run carefully in double harness, than the helpless-looking baby ones he had selected. Under her soft, babyish exterior Mrs. Beckington however had the quality of common sense developed to a remarkable degree, and when she married, the warm love she bore her husband seemed to bring her an intuition of his nature quite beyond what a cleverer woman might have reasoned. Instead of trying to wean him from his former tastes, she became his devoted companion. Living in his pursuits and ideas, learning to ride straight in the Meadowbrook hunt, to take an interest in yachts and horse-racing, to play billiards by the hour, and last, but not least, to understand her husband's desire for other companionship than her own—for men and tobacco smoke. Her house was the gathering ground for her husband's bachelor friends, who voted it the jolliest one in the city.

One cold, snowy night in December Mr. and Mrs. Beckington were for once alone. They sat talking by the fire for some time after dinner and then went into the billiard room, which was a long addition built on an adjoining lot. The walls were panelled in hard wood, and the polished floor was bare of rugs save for a huge tiger-skin before the tiled fireplace, where a bright fire burned. A leather divan ran all around the walls, and there was little else in the way of furniture except the big table and a few comfortable chairs.

A pretty woman never looks prettier than at billiards ; and Mrs. Beckington had on a bright scarlet gown that lit up her little dark face, and as she moved to and fro the red dashes of her bright silk caught and were reflected a hundred times in the polished surfaces about her. Her face wore a look of intense absorption as she took aim. Her husband, in contrast, played hastily and brilliantly, the play of an experienced man not quite sure of the steadiness of his nerves and hand.

"One, two," she cried at last. "I believe I am going to win. There!"

as she sent her ball whirling across the table—"beaten by two points— now how do you feel?"

Her face was lit up like a little, soft, dark rose by the excitement ; she was bewitchingly pretty, and her husband moved around the table to where she stood and put his arm around her lovingly.

" I think my wife is the cleverest little woman in the world! Shall we try another game? "

" In just a moment," she answered, nestling against his shoulder. " Clarence " — with great eagerness — " aren't you glad you married a girl who can beat you at billiards? "

" Indeed I am, dear. When I was a bachelor, on snowy nights like this, when none of the men came around and I was too lazy to go up to the club, the butler would come and play with me. Old Thomas taught me when I was a boy; he is a very good player, but it rather lowered my self-esteem to have my own butler give me every other game just as though I was still fourteen years old.''

''So you think I am an improvement on Thomas, do you?'' laughed Mrs. Beckington.

''Oh, yes, a lot. You don't know how awfully amusing you look when you play—your eyes get so bright and your hair tips so becomingly sideways.''

''Clarence, you are a mean tease.'' And darting away from him, she playfully poked her cue at the middle of his immaculate shirt front.

''Stop, Bertha; you'll bend the cue.''

He reached out his long arm to catch the provoking little red fairy, but she danced out of his reach, and for a few minutes they chased each other around the table, until Bertha sank into a chair breathless.

When peace was restored and she had recovered her breath, nothing would content her but that they must play again. It was the first time she had ever beaten her husband, and she wanted to see if she could repeat her success.

Mr. Beckington was secretly almost as much pleased as she was ; he would go around for days telling how his wife had beaten him at billiards, for he was tremendously proud of her success in all sports. He pretended, however, to consider her conduct most undignified.

"Now, Bertha, don't you dare beat me again," he said, shaking his cue at her as they began a new game. "If you do I shall get out the marriage service and read you your proper duty toward your husband."

"My proper duty towards my husband," throwing back her head in glee and showing all her little even teeth, "is to beat him if I can."

"Just so, my dear; see if you can again."

They were chalking their cues afresh when the door opened and a middle-aged man entered with all the freedom of an *habitué* of the house. He had a thin, characteristic face and sharp little eyes, and his spare, straight figure was carried with the precision of a martinet.

"Hello, Gordon White, make yourself at home," called Mr. Beckington, shaking the newcomer's hand. "Don't speak to Bertha or you will upset her; she has been getting an aim for the last half hour."

Bertha smilingly held out her little hand, which Mr. White, with the air of an old beau, raised to his lips.

"You don't mind if we go on, do you?" she said. "You know you may smoke."

No, Mr. White did not mind their going on. In his phlegmatic existence there were probably no happier hours than when, curled up in a corner in the Beckingtons' house, he watched Mrs. Beckington flitting around. He drew a chair up to the fire, lit a cigar and leaned back, blowing rings of smoke in perfect contentment.

The game went on, and as he sat watching the husband and wife his keen eyes expressed a degree of affection that would have surprised their owner, who prided himself on his stoical demeanor.

The capture of Gordon White, one

of her husband's most intimate friends and an inveterate clubman, was one of the brightest plumes in Mrs. Beckington's cap. He was wont to say he had never supposed there was a better place than his own corner at the club until Clarence was married.

"When I went to the wedding," he would exclaim pathetically, "I thought—there, I have lost another friend—another house full of women and tea."

For a long time he would accept none of his friend's invitations to come and meet his wife; finally, when he met Mrs. Beckington he thought her a fraud and kept a keen watch upon her; he could not believe that she really liked her husband's friends, smoking, and playing billiards. When he came to the conclusion that she was sincere he settled into her devoted henchman, and had even been known upon one occasion to offer to escort her to an afternoon reception.

As he watched her pretty red figure flitting around the table a feeling of age and loneliness crept over him, and his thoughts were drifting away in a manner which he would have characterized as "beastly sentimental, you know," when the door opened again to admit another visitor. This time a very young man of huge, athletic figure, his square, clean-cut face surmounted by a shock of light hair that to his great annoyance could never be made to assume the semi-fashionable baldness. This mane of hair and a nice pair of gray eyes were his most characteristic features. Not a clever man, Jim Ashley—rather a commonplace, clean, sweet boy whom every one felt confidence in.

"Good evening, Jim," they all called with delightful informality.

"Good evening—how is the game —how many are you?"

Mrs. Beckington excitedly gave him a left handshake.

"I won the last game and I'm crazy to beat this. I'm a point ahead."

The two outsiders immediately fell to betting upon her chances. They stood beside the table, eagerly watching every point, and applauded wildly as Bertha made a brilliant stroke and scored. She had beaten, and sank into a chair exhausted with her triumph. Her pulses beat wildly with the excitement of the game, and she was flushed and hot. Her husband brought a smoking-jacket and wrapped it around her warm neck and arms with loverlike devotion, making her look like a pretty child with her little curly head and mignonne face peeping out of the depths of big collar. Gordon White brought his cigar and sat down on the divan beside her, refusing the charms of a game for once, and the two others began to play again.

It would probably have been a great blow to Gordon White's pride had he known that Mrs. Beckington's great reason for liking him was because she thought him quite an old gentleman. The paternal air which he affected toward her went better with his well-preserved sixty years than he had any idea. He leaned toward her now in a manner expressive of the greatest interest in their *tête-à-tête.*

"Tell me, my dear young lady," he said pompously, "what have you been doing this long winter day?"

"Oh, I've been doing such a lot of

things. Which reminds me, I have been so hoping all day that you would come in this evening, for there is something I want you to do specially for me ; will you?"

"Anything," he answered sentimentally.

As he spoke the two men looked up from their game, and as Bertha, settling back in her chair, answered sweetly, "I want you to buy me a doll," there was a laugh from their region that told they had been listening.

"I don't mind your scoffing one bit," White called to them good-naturedly. "If Mrs. Beckington wants a doll I will certainly get her one. My dear young lady, won't your husband let you have a doll?"

It took some time for Mrs. Beckington to explain that she did not want to play with a doll, but that she was one of the patronesses of the Children's Aid Society, and intended asking every man she knew to give her a toy for the Christmas tree. She very particularly impressed upon Mr. White that he must go and buy the doll himself, so that he would really be doing something for the poor.

"Bless her kind little heart!" thought White, as he took out his notebook and wrote in a pretty cramped hand, "Buy a doll." He chuckled to himself as he closed the book on the entry, which looked so queerly among a list of bets and other essentially masculine doings.

Mrs. Beckington suddenly turned to her husband with an alert, quick movement, like a little bird.

"Clarence, do you think Mr. White would like to hear about the girl bachelor?" she said anxiously.

Her husband laughed; he was used to his wife's fresh enthusiasms. As soon as she came home from her calls that afternoon she had begun about her new acquaintance, and had talked to him all the time they were dressing for dinner, and all through dinner and all the time they were sitting by the fire, and until they began their game. He felt quite willing to hear it all over again, however, and was sure White would want to know all about the girl bachelor.

"What is a girl bachelor?" queried White.

Mr. Ashley too was interested; he stopped playing and joined them.

"What is it? I too am anxious to be enlightened. What's a girl bachelor? Is White a girl bachelor?"

Mr. White glared at him crossly.

"I should think it was one of those

dudes in trained frock coats one sees on Fifth Avenue about five o'clock in the afternoon," he retorted gruffly.

"Do let me speak," said Mrs. Beckington pathetically.

She always declared that men talked so much she was never able to get in a word in her own house. However, for once there were no more interruptions, while she told them all about the girl bachelor.

Briefly, her narrative was to the effect that Dorothy Mason, a young lady who will be properly introduced in the coming chapters, had been having her portrait painted, and Mrs. Mason had called in the afternoon to take Bertha up to the studio to let her see how successful the picture was. Bertha had admired the portrait, but still more the artist herself. A long campaign of receptions had been planned, but the two ladies let the afternoon slip by while they lingered in the studio, and when Bertha reached home she was bubbling with enthusiasm concerning the charms and talents of Miss Craig, who painted so well, and was so delightful.

When at last she stopped talking, Mr. White looked down on her fluffy head with an air of decided amusement.

"And may I ask," he said, "is this interesting girl bachelor a gay young thing between forty and fifty, whose portraits it is as much a charity to buy as the dolls for your Christmas tree? Does she do such nice illustrations— only they won't sell?"

For reply Bertha walked across the room and got the last number of the *Century*, which contained one of Miss Craig's illustrations. It was a clever, crisp drawing, certainly not amateurish, and the men's opinion of her *protégée* rose at once.

"Her portrait of Dorothy is splendidly broad and all that sort of thing, like Chase, and she must make lots of money, for her studio was hung with tapestry ever so much more beautiful than what we have, and she gave us such good tea. Oh, it was all so charming and original, so different from the way we stupid people live," she said regretfully.

Mr. Ashley and Mr. White had not been paying strict attention to the last part of her remarks; they had been whispering in the most undignified, schoolboyish fashion.

"We don't doubt that her studio is superb, but was she very emancipated? White wants to know," said Ashley mischievously.

"I don't," growled White indignantly.

" Yes, he does ; he wants to know if
she has short hair and if she wears
trousers.   He says he has heard of a
woman artist who did."

Certainly Miss Craig's pretty ears
ought to have burned at the amount
of interest she was exciting.   Mrs.
Beckington took her new acquaintance seriously ; she would allow no
sarcasms or light suggestions.   Short
hair ! She described with much
warmth the prettiness of Miss Craig's
hair! Trousers! She scorned the idea,
and went off into an admiring description of the dainty gown in which
the artist had received her.   She finally routed the scoffing men by declar-
ing that she not only dressed to perfection, but that Mrs. Mason had said
that she made all her gowns herself.

"Mrs. Beckington," cried Ashley in mock devotion, falling down on one knee before her, "I implore you to introduce me to her. Do you think she could make dress shirts? Heavens! what a saving. White, you can't have her ; I spoke first."

"Don't worry, my boy," said the astute bachelor ; "I'll never marry any woman unless she can make high hats and patent-leather shoes."

Mrs. Beckington felt a little angry. She had quite fallen in love with the little maiden who was so simple and natural and did the honors of her big studio with such quiet dignity. She did not like her friends made fun of.

"I should have thought you would have been more sympathetic," she said, glaring at the three laughing faces. "She is the most charming girl I ever saw, and you seem to think that a woman who has any brains must be an ugly little old maid! Miss Craig isn't an old maid and she never will be. As we were coming away I said to Dorothy that it seemed funny such a nice girl hadn't married, and she quite snapped at me. She said, ' Oh, Miss Craig is a girl bachelor;' that's where I got the name. It just suits her and I think it so pretty."

There was warmth about Mrs. Beckington's partisanship of everything, from dolls for a Christmas tree to the wounded reputation of her friends, which, while it might not always carry conviction as to the justice of her cause, at any rate reflected her goodness of heart. She was given to enthusiasms that were not by any means short-lived. Her healthful nature seemed to feel by intuition the true worth of those with whom she was thrown, and if she had a good many intimate friends, certainly no one could accuse her of lacking in faithfulness to any of them. Nor do I think she was an exception in this; the theory that women are little cats, purring to each other's faces and biting behind each other's backs, is certainly worn threadbare, and the comic papers that fill their columns about women's jealousies and small meannesses would find their ardent friendships and enthusiasms much more amusing.

"I'll not tell you another thing about her," said Mrs. Beckington, with a pout. "You sha'n't any of you know her, and Dorothy Mason and I will keep her all to ourselves. Oh, just one thing more"—recollecting herself: "my brother Philip knows her; I met him going in just as we were coming away."

They were all startled by a voice from the doorway:

"The saying about the devil is trite," it called, "but since I hear my name you might as well tell me what it is all about. Good evening—how comfortable you all look—Bertha, as usual, posing as an angel in a cloud of tobacco-smoke." The owner of the voice entered the room and joined the group, shaking hands with the men and kissing Mrs. Beckington affectionately.

"How did you come to know her?" they all cried.

"Who, Bertha? Met her when she was a baby."

"No, not Bertha; the girl bachelor."

"What are you all talking about? What an extraordinary reception! If I did not know the ways of this erratic household I should think you were all slightly insane. Who is a girl bachelor, and what do you mean?"

"Oh, it's all my fault," said Bertha. "Mrs. Mason took me to Miss Craig's studio this afternoon, and I have been telling them about her. A girl like her, who earns her own living, is called a girl bachelor, you see."

As she spoke she felt that her brother was displeased; a shade passed across his dark face, which was, by one of those curious family likenesses, very similar in feature, but entirely different in character and expression.

Separated by ten years of age, in Philip's lighter moods, and in a certain winsome charm that he had not entirely outgrown with his early manhood, they seemed much alike, but in his more thoughtful, deeper moments one would scarcely have guessed them to be of the same family.

"My dear sister," he said gravely, "don't you think it is rather hard that because a young woman is so unfortunate as to have to earn her own living that she must be called by a slang name?"

Perhaps he felt his tone more reproving than he intended, for he added:

"Were you going to Mrs. Howard's? I stopped in there on my way up and she asked me if you wouldn't be around."

Mrs. Beckington saw that he did not wish to further discuss the young artist. Womanlike, she immediately wondered why not.

The evening had slipped by so quickly that she had forgotten about her engagement at Mrs. Howard's "small and early." The carriage had been waiting for some time; she declared she must go, and hurried out of the room to get her *sortie de bal.* "Who is going with me?" she said, coming back in a moment and sticking her head in through the door. "Clarence has such a cold I can't possibly martyrize him."

The three other men started toward her; but no! she could not take them all. She finally decided on Mr. Ashley, who was still of an age to enjoy a dance, and they went skipping down the hall together gayly, Mr. Beckington watching his wife's little figure until the door closed.

"Bring her back safely, Jim," he called after them.

CHAPTER II

The three men sat for some time around the fire and smoked in silence. Now that Mrs. Beckington was gone, they assumed easier attitudes and their faces relaxed into that calm blankness that men allow themselves when they know each other intimately and have nothing in particular to say. They were essentially men who had seen life, had lived, enjoyed, sinned and suffered. Gordon White, older by twenty years than the others, and who in general society appeared only a little their senior, dropped back, now that his face was deprived of its usually alert air, into a much older looking man. There were those who wondered what his real life had been. A great traveller, a bookworm, a pleasant friend and companion, modest to a fault, punctilious in dress and manner, a bright, keen wit—whatever may have been the stormy passages of his past, he had kept his own secrets well, and his quiet, reserved face told no tales. Men in their lives live many characters, and perhaps we have met Gordon White in really the happiest and finest period of his life, when the sting is softening out of his sharp speeches and he is mellowing down into his last part, that of an old beau dancing attendance upon pretty Mrs. Beckington.

The other men were still young, and there had existed between them a warm friendship since their college days, when they had shared each other's rooms, belongings, and pranks. It is out of date, I know, and rather savors of the Elizabethan age to talk of men loving each other, but these two men loved each other with an affection which was no less real because our age of broadcloth and starch does not lend itself to the show of as much feeling as that in which the greatest mind of English literature indited sonnets to Mr. W. H. They knew each other's lives for good or evil, with no reservations, and as Philip's little sister grew up out of her short frocks, Clarence was always held up to her as the criterion of all that was excellent and fascinating, and on her wedding day Mrs. Beckington could very well have said that her husband was her first and only love. If a bond had been needed to cement the two men closer together, it

was formed by their interests center-
ing in her lovable little person.

Philip Herford sat brooding and
looking into the fire, his brow knitted
over his deep-set eyes as he thought.
He was one of those men who are
handsome from a fine presence rather
than from regularity of feature. The
word charming seldom applies to a
man's appearance without some reser-
vation of effeminacy, but Philip Herford was charming from strength and
magnetism. His face was intellectual
and his eyes thoughtful under his deep
brows. He liked the society of artists
and literary people, the society of
London and Paris—his friends were
as the sands of the sea. Now, as he
sat thinking, his face wore a look of
melancholy, and his mouth and chin
were square and strong in contrast to
his soft dark eyes, settled into grim

determination. His cigar went out, but he did not heed it, and leaned his head on his hand as though in physical weariness, staring into the fire. The room was quiet, save for an occasional falling of coal in the grate. Finally White roused himself from the comfortable corner in which he had been nearly asleep.

"I must be getting along," he said; "there's a meeting up at the club that I ought to get to before to-morrow. Good night, Philip; good night, Beckington." And the little bachelor was on his way to his favorite haunt.

"Nice fellow, old White," said Philip as the door closed behind him. "How he wears. When I was about twelve years old I can remember his looking just as he does now." He spoke more from a desire to break the long silence than from any interest in what he was saying.

"I wonder if it is still snowing," said Clarence, going to the window. "If it is, the horses will be buried, Bertha is staying so late." He drew the curtain, letting a flood of moonlight into the room. The snow had ceased, the sky was full of glittering stars; it was one of those cold, glittering nights that come after a storm. As he looked out into the white street, which on the morrow would be a mass of dirty-brown wheel tracks, it brought to his mind his college days and the cold winter nights on the hills of New Haven. "It makes me think of college," he said, wondering what was the matter with his gloomy friend.

Philip arose and came to the window, looking out into the moonlight over his shoulder.

"Yes," he said, "the snow always makes me think of college too, and our nights on the bob runners down those long icy hills. Talk about toboggan slides and skeeing and every other kind of sport, they don't come anywhere near our old sleds."

He was trying to throw off his black mood. Lighting his cigar again, he lounged among the comfortably piled pillows that Mr. White had left, preparing to spend an hour in reminiscence and small talk. Mr. Beckington, however, knew his nature too well not to realize that there was something wrong with him.

"Is there anything the matter, old man?" he said, still looking out of the window. "You haven't been yourself for the last few days—I suppose it's the old story."

It was a brutal way of speaking,

but he was trying not to appear too much interested in his friend's mood. The words jarred on Philip. "The old story," he thought; "what an epitaph on a love affair—an old story ! When the story that is so new to us at first gets to be an old story it is old enough to be buried in its faded memories."

There was a chapter in Philip Herford's life so well guarded that the world knew nothing of it, a chapter opened to only one person, his old college friend who had been his confidant and adviser. It was an old story now. In Philip's senior year the entire college had been turned upside down with enthusiasm and excitement over the fact that Margaret Fremiet, the great actress, was going to appear as Portia for three nights in New Haven. What fortunes were spent in flowers, what sums of money squandered for seats in the front row, what heartburns and jealousies, would fill a volume. The two friends went together to the play, and had the good fortune to be presented to Madame Fremiet afterward. She was then about thirty-five, in the very prime of her rich beauty, full of fascination and charm. She seemed not only to awaken Philip's admiration, but to fill some want in his essentially artistic nature. He loved her, and in his crazy boyish zeal he told her so. It was an altogether unforeseen chapter of events. Philip Herford, dreamy, artistic, offered Margaret Fremiet his devotion with all the strength of a first love. But there was one side of the question, however, that he had never entertained—his love was returned. Marriage between them was impossible; Margaret's husband was living, and absolutely refused to grant her a divorce. Years went by; they loved each other with devotion, but no breath of scandal had ever been raised between them. Their acquaintance had naturally been at glimpses and long periods, and for the two past years before this story opens, Margaret Fremiet had been in Europe winning fresh laurels. She was now playing in New York, her farewell engagement, it was whispered. It was a strange coil: she had not changed, Philip had not changed, and yet in the two years that she had been away new interests, new ties had crept into his life. He did not feel their strength until this very afternoon, when he found himself murmuring words of love to another woman, words which he had suddenly checked. Horrified at their utterance and his disloyalty to Margaret, he had left the girl quickly, half dazed, half stunned by the revelation of his feeling which had swept over him with blinding suddenness. When he reached his rooms he found a letter from Margaret; the one thing for which they had waited so long had happened—her husband was dead.

The hideous farce of the whole thing seemed burned into Philip's brain. He was a faith-breaker, and, worst of all, some one had to be sacrificed. He could not bear the penalty of his weakness alone. In honor he was bound to Margaret Fremiet, and without hesitation he sat down and wrote in reply to her letter; but the thought of the morrow, of the gentle heart that he would have to break, came over him with a sense of physical suffering. He looked up at Clarence now with an air that baffled his friend's scrutiny.

"Do you remember my first boyish raptures over Margaret?" he said with a quiet smile. "I wanted to tell you the first of all." He stood up and held out his hand with a winning gesture. "I am sure you will congratulate me," he said; "her husband is dead; we are going to be married."

"I'm awfully glad, Philip," said Mr. Beckington, shaking his hand warmly.

Inwardly, however, he was rather disappointed. Much as he had always admired Margaret Fremiet, he had never quite understood Philip's infatuation for her, and since his own marriage he had hoped that the link between them was dying a natural death, and that in time Philip would marry some good little girl who would

be all the world to him. A silence
fell between the two friends, as though
there was nothing more to say.

"Well, I must be going along; good
night," Philip said at last, carelessly.
With his hand on the door, however,
he turned. "There was something I
wasn't going to say, but I will," he
went on quietly. "I wish, Clarence,
that you would ask Bertha to be kind
to that little Miss Craig, the artist. I
have been going there a good deal
lately and she is very much alone in
the world. There is some trouble
hanging over her just now and a
woman friend might help her."
Then, as if Mr. Beckington had not
taken in the full sense of his words, he
looked at him earnestly. "It will be
a reparation if Bertha will be kind to
her"—then he was gone.

Mr. Beckington sat down by the

fire again and was so deep in thought that he did not hear the door open when his wife, all rosy and cold from the biting air, came softly in and put her hands over his eyes. Of course it was with the greatest difficulty that he could guess who had that tiny pair of hands, but even when they had been kissed and his wife perched comfortably on the broad arm of his chair, his face was still grave.

" Why, you old bear, you don't seem a bit glad that I've come home. Were you doing a little thinking while I was out of the house so I couldn't disturb you? How very solemn you look."

Mrs. Beckington had been brought up not to ask questions; her brother had come in looking glum and grave, and now she found her husband in the same mood. She did not ask what was the matter, but waited to be told, and I can say in favor of this system that generally she was told.

"Philip is going to be married, my dear," said Mr. Beckington, secretly thinking that not all the actresses or any other celebrated beauties were quite as fine as his own sweet wife.

"Who is he going to marry?" she asked.

"Margaret Fremiet."

"Gracious goodness! what an exalted marriage! She's awfully nice, though. But, Clarence, why should Philip look so unhappy when he's going to be married? Did you look like that when you were engaged?"

Mr. Beckington roared.

"I tried to keep up a pretty cheerful exterior when I was with you," he said, "but I can assure you that at other times I looked much more unhappy than Philip."

CHAPTER III.

Alida Craig was sitting on the
top of a high ladder working at a big
stained-glass cartoon that was tacked
on one side of her studio wall.   A
large piece of tapestry and some bric-
à-brac which had been taken down to
make way for the cartoon were piled
in an untidy heap on the floor, giving
the room the air of a workshop.
There were some very good pieces of
tapestry on the walls, the fruit of long
searches in the back streets of Paris in
her student days, and the furniture
was a motley collection of chairs and
tables, many of which had been bought
in the most dilapidated condition and

then polished and put in order as ready money and opportunity offered. There were book shelves filled, alas ! not with those sets of polite literature which no gentleman's library is without, but with worn half-calf and vellum volumes, picked up on the quays as she loitered along in the sunshine, and odd volumes of her favorite authors bought from time to time. Although it was late in the afternoon the big north window still let in a flood of light shining down on the sleek brown head of the owner of these multifarious and original belongings.

As she sat on the top of the ladder in a long blue work-apron, with her heavy hair unfastened and hanging in a thick plait down her back, she might have been taken for a little girl, she looked so thin and young and childlike.   As she worked she kept singing over and over to herself the faint, pathetic air of Berlioz:

> "Once there was a King of Thule,
> True he was and brave."

A model, an oval-faced, angelic-looking creature clad in thin Greek drapery, stood on the platform.   In the intentness of keeping her pose her face assumed an expression of purity and sweetness that would have astonished those who saw her snapping black eyes and bewildering kickings in the front row of a comic opera chorus at night.   Sometimes the girl would talk slang and nonsense, of the balls she had been to and of the compliments she had received, chatter which Alida scarcely heard in the absorption of her work.   Miss Matilda Tremaine was known in private life as

Jenny Brady. Her early life had been passed as the daughter of a small politician who kept a liquor saloon in the Bowery. She was of the Bowery still, in a certain rough honesty. She knew the world and everything in it at fourteen. She was pretty, vulgar, uneducated. Beyond the first row of the chorus she could never hope to climb. Once, in a state of financial depression, she had taken to posing, and although she was not in need now, she was always ready to sit for Alida, whose innocence and guilelessness were a source of profound astonishment to her. Her devotion to the little artist "who did angels and didn't know anything" was profound, and Alida would have been surprised to know that her name was held in love and veneration by three of the friskiest chorus girls in the city.

" Why, she believes my hair was born auburn," she would often say to her companions.

Lately Jenny Brady had constituted herself the guardian angel of the little artist. Her only theory of life could probably be explained in " men are villains." From her youngest days the villain side had been uppermost in her experience. Philip Herford's face, like that of every other notable man in town, was perfectly familiar to her; she knew of his frequent visits to Alida's studio, and as the winter wore away she continually wondered what the end might be. If at fourteen Jenny Brady had known everything, at twenty-two, the age to which she now answered, her information had been increased by a prodigious mass of gossiping detail. Did she not know more of people's private lives than their own immediate friends—nay, even sometimes more than they knew themselves? If she knew Philip Herford, did she not also know Margaret Fremiet? Had she not been a Roman vestal for a season in her company? She watched Alida's face during the winter budding into new beauty and happiness each day. Everything seemed going well, and yet Jenny had a decided feeling that there was going to be a tragedy somewhere, possibly because of her "villain" theory. Her feeling was that if anything did happen *she would act.*

"It's getting dark, you'd better stop posing," said Alida, getting down from the ladder. " You haven't been talking this afternoon, Jenny; have you got a headache?"

She spoke half dreamily, walking

backward across the room, gazing at the cartoon with glimmered eyes. Her little lithe body was poised with the subtle grace, almost lost among women, of one who was absolutely unconscious of herself, and was used to perfect physical freedom. Her long oval face was full of character, and the strong marked chin gave it a strength which belied the softness of the round contours and the childlike expression of her eyes—deep-set gray eyes, under level artist's brows, that flashed with changing expression when she spoke and illuminated her face into rare intellectual beauty. As the clock struck four she took off her apron, tidied up the room with a few wild strokes, pinned a big piece of cheesecloth over the cartoon, and rushed up the stairway to her little bedroom to tidy her hair and get into a presentable dress. Her belt was just fastened, and she was getting a last glimpse of herself in a long glass, as a woman will who regards her appearance, when the door-bell rang and she rushed down to open it.

"I didn't know whether you'd like to see me so soon again," said her visitor, stooping her tall head to kiss Alida, "but I have got so used to coming here in the afternoon that now the portrait is done I want to come just the same."

"Indeed, I am glad you came. Take off your things, Dorothy, and we will have some tea. I have just finished working."

Dorothy Mason was one of the type of big, well-groomed, healthy girls that are such a delight to the eyes and the soul. She dropped her things in a heap on the divan, drew the long gloves off her hands, which were sparkling with rings, and dived into her pocket for a bonbon box, which she offered to Alida. Her admiration for Alida was unbounded. Spoiled and petted and brought up all her life to look at the world from the point of money and the position it brought, the little artist girl with her sweet, low voice, correct ways and dainty womanliness had completely overthrown the narrow and Philistine ideas that Dorothy's parents had so carefully inculcated. Only eighteen, she was little more than a big little girl, and was just at the age to adore an older woman and be easily influenced by her.

"May I make the tea? You're tired ; let me," she said with a superior air.

"Oh, I'm not a bit tired; I've been

sitting up on that ladder until I am glad to move around. Do you think you would spoil your regal garments if you came with me into the kitchen? It's Chloe's afternoon out, and I have promised to make a pudding for dinner. It will only take a few minutes, and then we will toast some muffins."

She led the way as she spoke, to the tiny kitchen of the apartment, a diminutive room fitted with a little range and tubs. A shining kettle hissed upon the fire and a burnished "*batterie de cuisine*" hung on the wall. There were some thriving geraniums too in the window, where they caught the sunshine. Alida took great pride in these thrifty plants and always spoke of them as her conservatory.

"What a dear place," cried Dorothy enthusiastically. "It looks like a doll's kitchen. How cunning the shining kettles are, hung up by their tails. Our kitchen is perfectly horrid down in the basement, and the cook is so cross that I wouldn't go down there for anything."

"Do you think it is a pretty room?" said Alida, as she walked around collecting her dishes and materials for the pudding.

She was very much pleased, for Alida, for all her childlike deportment seeming, had the most decided views regarding the decoration of the three rooms that formed her "house." She was far from believing in the theory that presents a "cinnamon pink to a dying Chinaman," but she believed that a kitchen had just as much right to be pretty and attractive in its own limits as any other room. She had brought the shining copper casseroles over from Paris quite as much because they made an artistic background for her big black servant as because they were good to cook in. The little place boasted only one chair, and Dorothy sitting in it before the range filled up most of the room. Alida rolled up her sleeves, tied Chloe's enormous apron around her slender waist, and began sifting flour and beating eggs in a businesslike manner. Dorothy sat tipping back in the deal chair, her mouth filled with raisins, and indulged in a rhapsody concerning the wonderfulness of the young woman whose talents included stained-glass windows, painting portraits, making her own clothes and puddings. Alida was used to the girl's admiration—so used that generally she simply changed the subject by diverting her friend's mind into some other channel. There had been growing up in her mind during the past weeks a real love and interest in the big, amiable girl.

Perhaps Alida was really more tired than she thought, perhaps it was only a desire for a little sympathy, but as she mixed the eggs into the flour with the big spoon, her face wore a very grave and sweet expression.

" Dorothy, you mustn't envy me," she said. " Although I am awfully happy, it's taken years and years of hard work learning to do the things that you think so original. Do you know I would give it all, the best picture that I have ever painted, or shall paint, to be able to look back to the happy childhood that you are having? I never had any girlhood; it was all hard work and dingy studios. Do you remember talking the other day of the pretty things you were going to wear to the Patriarchs'? I really envied you. I am twenty-five and I've never been to a ball."

"Why, you dear little thing," cried Dorothy, bounding out of her chair and putting her arms around Alida, regardless of the flour and the pudding. "Haven't you really ever been to a ball?" Then in a tone of real sympathy: "Didn't you have a coming-out tea?"

"Coming-out tea! When I was your age I had one gown and two paint aprons. Chloe and I lived in a tiny apartment under an attic roof in Paris." She poured the beaten egg over the top of the pudding with reckless haste; the mention of the by-gone years disturbed her. "Coming-out tea!" she continued, putting the pudding in the oven; "I'd have been thankful for any kind of a tea. Although I'm so thin I've an enormous appetite, and most of the time I was positively hungry. Don't mind my getting excited over the recollection of it," she said apologetically.

"Mind?" There were positively tears in Dorothy's blue eyes. "You are so little and frail-looking that when you break out in that bitter way it makes me feel dreadfully. You ought to have had some one look after you; it's terrible for a girl to work so hard. Alida, were you ever engaged?" she said abruptly.

The pudding scarcely needed attention yet, but Alida stooped, opened the oven door, and turned the dish around before she answered.

"No, my dear."

"Not even the least little bit?" in a tone of disappointment.

"No, I'm afraid not even the least little bit. One of the men in the studio used to wash my paint brushes every afternoon. He was a big Englishman and painted very badly in the English way; he didn't even wash paint brushes well. I couldn't possibly have been in love with any one who did such awful work. I'm afraid I have been too busy to have had many romances."

"I've been engaged for two years," said Dorothy, with a grave air with which she had been told it was suitable to enter a ballroom. She seemed quite to fill the little room with pride and dignity.

"You! You're only eighteen," said Alida. Then she saw that Dorothy was really in earnest, and in a moment she was all sympathy and sweetness, and Dorothy, who for all her money

and position, English accent and dig-
.nified demeanor, was really at heart
only a schoolgirl, with many explanations and apologies, told a long story
that without its many digressions
would have run something like this:

When she had outgrown her pretty
baby-girl stage and was not yet big
enough to "come out," her mother
had sent her to a school in New
Haven to be "finished." It was one
of those silly fashionable schools
which with all the talk about modern
education still flourish. The girls vied
with each other in the possession of
luxurious toilet articles and under-
wear, and the literary standard was
principally that of the Duchess and
Dora Thorne. Dorothy's head was
filled with the manly heroes described
by those vacuous authors. At the
school's monthly receptions, at which

the girls were allowed to see their brothers and cousins, she fell, in her funny little girl way, desperately in love with a large and amiable young man who was the captain of the football team. She was such a child that she took the greatest pride in his being a sophomore, and felt that she could never have been in love with a mere freshman, as some of the girls were. She was large and developed for her age, and at fifteen was a practised coquette, her mind stored with romances, and yet under it all a warm, loving heart capable of enduring affection if it was really touched. The big sophomore grew to be a yet bigger senior, and he was more in love with her than she with him. Before his last term was out, in the profoundest secrecy these two, who had never met excepting under the eyes of a squad of teachers and some forty school-girls, were engaged.

Alida was a good deal surprised at the revelation. She knew her friend to be a great heiress, and the story savored to her of unpleasant complications.

"Doesn't even your mother know?" she said at last as Dorothy paused.

"No; do you suppose I was going to be engaged before I came out?" suddenly dropping from her romantic mood into calculating calmness. "Every one would have called us the babes in the wood, as they did Alice Larkin last year. No, indeed; it's such fun being secretly engaged, so exciting meeting for a moment on the stairs, or in the conservatory at a dance, and to have to pretend we aren't glad when we have been sent into dinner together. Oh, he's been so terribly jealous."

"You funny girl, one moment you are all for romance and the next you are so practical. I don't understand you one bit," said Alida.

Dorothy walked up and down the room excitedly. The romantic in her nature was strong. Lydia Languish no more truly sighed over the degeneracy of chivalry than this Fifth Avenue maiden. After the wild excitement, the makeshifts to get letters, the clandestine meetings, the way she had had to plan and manœuvre for the last two years, she felt that it would be too dull and commonplace to come down to being labelled engaged.

"I've worn my engagement ring around my neck for two years, and it would seem stupid to wear it on my finger now," she said, with withering scorn at Alida's commonplace advice. As she spoke she slipped a pretty diamond and sapphire ring off a ribbon that was under her dress and handed it to Alida. "Sapphire means constancy," said Dorothy. "You may read the inscription."

It was getting quite dark, but Alida knelt down before the kitchen fire and held the ring in a blaze of light.

"'Dorothy from J. A.,'" she said softly; "'November 1, 1890.' Dorothy, do you know anything about J. A.? I am older than you, dear, and although I don't know much about the world, I'm sure with your fortune you ought to be very careful."

Dorothy's face grew grave.

"Yes, dear, that's just it," she said. "Mamma has always told me how awful men are and that they would want to marry me for my money. Don't you think I can be pretty sure of a man who loved me when I was a schoolgirl with those awful half-long dresses and two thin pigtails?"

"Yes, dear, I think you could; and if J. A. is Mr. Ashley, who has been, I have been told, your devoted slave this winter, it is all right, but I'd tell my mother if I were you."

"I'll think about it," said Dorothy. Then she noticed how dark it was getting. The two girls had been so busy talking they had completely lost track of the time. Dorothy could not think of waiting to have any tea now, and she put on her jacket and straightened her hat before the little Venetian mirror in the studio. They went to the door together, and as Alida put up her face to kiss Dorothy good-by, she paused for a moment and then said:

"Dorothy, I never had many girl friends. It's so sweet in you to come and see me so often, and for you to tell me about your engagement, that it doesn't seem quite fair for me to say that I have never been engaged. Dorothy, dear, you mustn't be surprised if some day quite soon I tell you that I am engaged too."

Alida went back to the studio, which was now full of deep shadows. She drew the curtain over the big window, carried her little tea table close to the fire, and set the pretty brass kettle singing on the spirit lamp. Then she went to the kitchen, took the pudding, that was now a beautiful brown, out of the oven, and fussed around putting away the dishes that she had used. She was evidently waiting for some one, and when the door-bell rang she went to open the door with a slightly flushed face, perhaps from the heat of the fire.

Philip Herford came into the room

as he had been in the habit of coming in almost every day for several weeks past. As he said good-afternoon he stooped and kissed the tips of her soft fingers. She remembered the feeling of his lips and his beard brushing her hand for many days afterward. He went and sat in his accustomed seat by the fire and Alida made the tea. They did not speak. The girl was filled with a happy, still contentment that made her loath to break the silence. Their acquaintance had come about through Philip having bought one of her pictures, and, as was his way, he had sought out the artist, thinking perhaps that he might be of further service. He was as much amazed to discover the author of his picture in this little brown-haired girl living in her studio and work, attended by the faithful Chloe, as though she had been

an enchanted princess in a fairy
tower. Their acquaintance might
have never got beyond the formal
stage had not a man—one of those
odious, well-fed creatures who consider that because a woman works for
her living she is common prey for
their evil tongues and malice—given
vent in Philip's hearing to the malicious report that a well-known artist,
whose style resembled Alida's principally because they had admired—and
studied under—the same master,
painted all her pictures.

Philip rose to her vindication. He
was powerful enough to stop the
man's lying tongue, but the rumor of
course had reached the girl's ears, and
it was one of the darkest times of her
life. Then, for the first time in her
lonely, parentless existence, she had a
protector, and a strong one. They

became friends. She was so away from the world, so wrapped in her work and dreams, more protected by them, indeed, than by the most be-jewelled dowager of the Patriarchs', that their friendship moved along as calmly as though no question of sex had been raised between them. They read books together, talked poetry and of the paintings of the Louvre and Florence, never of life of which the girl knew nothing; all was of art and the beautiful things of which she knew so much.

Then one afternoon, when Philip's calls in the dusk had been getting more and more frequent, something happened—how they never knew. A touching of hands unconsciously over a book, and Philip broke out in a mad babble of love words, and the girl heard him, and her heart sang and she put up her face like a child to be kissed, and loved him forever. It was only yesterday, but as she sat beside the little tea table watching the steam pour out of the kettle, she felt as though they had always loved each other, and that all the sorrow and bitterness of her early years was melted away. The tea was ready, and she put the sugar in the cups and carefully lifted the teapot. Philip roused himself and laid his hand over hers on the handle.

"I don't want any tea, Alida, I want to talk to you," he said.

"Yes?" smiling.

"I am going away, dear."

"Isn't it very sudden?—you didn't think of going yesterday."

"When I said I was going away, I did not mean I was going on a journey. Alida"—his face contracted with pain—"I am going to tell you something, dear"—he stopped—"I love you," he said passionately, "I have said it and nothing will make me unsay it."

Alida, wondering, came and knelt down by his chair.

"I told you that I loved you yesterday," she said with a little flush; "do you expect me to tell you so every day?"

Philip looked down into her little face. Her heart beat nervously with a foreboding of coming evil. He put his arm around her lovingly and laid one of his large, soft hands tenderly over her eyes as though to blot out his image as he spoke.

"Alida, dear, I shall never ask you to tell me so again. Never again shall I kiss you or hold your hands or even come here. I ought not to have spoken as I did yesterday." He could feel every nerve in the girl's soft body quiver with pain.

Then she raised her head and looked him full in the eyes. She had borne poverty, hunger, and cold, slights and disappointments; it had made her strong to endure suffering.

"Tell me, dear," she said.

"When I was a mere college lad I fell in love with a very lovely woman, a married woman. You know I am much older than you are, Alida, and of course a man of my age has many things in his past life. This lady is one of the best and noblest women I have ever known. Her husband has just died—do you realize that I can marry no one else, that I am bound to her by every tie of honor?"

"Yes." The word came dully through the girl's parched lips.

"Forgive me, Alida; forget that mad hour yesterday."

The girl rose from her knees; drawing her slender body up straight like a reed, her eyes flashed.

"No," she said, clinching her little hands together in passion. "Forgive you—what for? For giving me the happiest hours of my life? Forget what you said yesterday—no! that is my half hour, all that I shall have to live on all my life. You may marry whom you will, but that half hour you loved me, you were mine." The flash died out as suddenly as it had come; her face grew white again, she put out her hand with a pathetic movement of weariness, steadying herself against the back of a chair. "You mustn't mind so, Philip; it's not so hard for me as you think. I've never been very happy. I've been alone all

SHE DROPPED INTO A CHAIR, COVERED HER FACE WITH HER HANDS, AND SOBBED. (P. 73.)

my life. I am afraid I am not like other girls who have homes and people to love them—no one has ever loved me but Chloe and you." Her voice broke into a sob; she pushed the heavy masses of hair away from her forehead. "Now I have only Chloe."

"Alida, you will break my heart—don't you realize—don't tempt me, dear."

"Tempt you?—no. The man I love will do what is right. You must go now."

She held up her hand to say good-by; the ghost of a smile played around her mouth.

"Good-by."

"Good-by."

Her courage gave out at last; she dropped into a chair, covered her face with her hands, and sobbed.

"I cannot let you go," she said.

Philip came back ; he knelt down by her chair in the dark, he passed his hands over her hair and eyes and hands and kissed the folds of her dress.

" Good-by, my dear little love," he said, and then left her.

CHAPTER IV

Madame Fremiet sat in her apartment at the Plaza reading a letter that she certainly must have known by heart, for she had read it many times already. Her eyes would stray out of the window with its attractive vista of the Park drive, and then she would read the letter over again. She examined the paper on which it was written, scrutinized the handwriting, and even laid it up against the glass to see the water-mark. All her efforts, however, were unavailing; the paper bore the common mark of Marcus Ward & Co., Belfast. The handwriting was a woman's ordinary running hand and gave no clue to the station or character of the writer. Ordinarily the recipient of a letter has only to turn to the end of the last page to find out who the writer is, but in this case it was different—it was anonymous. Margaret had received so many in the course of her life she was rather surprised to find she was so disturbed over this one. It read:

"My Dear Madame Fremiet:

"You will pardon the liberty of my addressing you in this abrupt manner, but I think you ought to know that your devoted admirer, Mr. Herford, has during your absence in Europe been paying a great deal of attention to another young lady. As she is an orphan, living by herself, with but few friends, I have taken this opportunity to clear up her position regarding Mr. Herford, as it may be a source of great unhappiness to

her in the future.   Please believe that
not malicious intentions but a sincere
love for the young lady in question,
who is Miss Alida Craig, an artist
whose studio is in the Sherburne
Building, prompts me to write you.
I am also a sincere admirer of your
great talents and noble character.
"Believe me,
"Very sincerely,
"UNKNOWN."

Madame Fremiet finally rose as if
to shake off the sting of the words.
She threw the note in the fire and
began to dress.   Even in the glare of
the afternoon sun which poured hotly
into the room she was still a very
handsome woman.   Her face was
unwrinkled, and the neck and shoulders that rose from the billowy lace
of her dainty dressing jacket were as
fair as a girl's.   As she stood in front
of the glass twisting up her hair, which

was heavy and abundant, she laughed, turning herself around on her toes. It was so absurd to think of Philip Herford caring for any other woman. Had she not been his first love? Was he not the king of all good men in her eyes? Had they not loved each other and been separated all these years without the shadow of changing between them? She laughed at the letter, and still it stung her. She dressed quickly without the assistance of her maid, twisting her hair up in a coil that characterized the beauty of her profile and the poise of her head. Then she put on a plain street dress, and, as she always did when anything was on her mind, and which probably accounted largely for the remarkable preservation of her beauty, went out for a walk, thinking that the cool fresh air would clear away the troubles of her mind. The color rose in her cheeks as she walked along, making her look almost girlish in her simple dress. People turned to look at her, she was so handsome and walked in such a free, graceful way, unmindful of anything but the enjoyment of physical exercise. She had not gone many blocks before she stopped. She had been trying to recollect in a dim way where she had heard the name of Miss Craig before, and as she passed the Masons' house the "correlation of ideas," as Herbert Spencer would call it, suddenly became complete. Was not Dorothy Mason's portrait being painted by Miss Craig? Madame Fremiet immediately turned up the Masons' steps and rang the bell, and had the good fortune to find Mrs. Mason in the parlor with her bonnet on, just ready to go out to a meeting of one of the hundred societies with useless objects to which she belonged. She was chairman of the meeting, but she let it wait for a few minutes' chat with Madame Fremiet.

Madame Fremiet did not know exactly why she had come, or just what she intended to do regarding the anonymous letter, or what use she would make of the Masons' connection with and knowledge of Miss Craig. Had Mrs. Mason not been going out she would probably have sat around for a while, talked of their thousand friends and the mutual chit-chat that women have in common, and finally, bringing the conversation around to Dorothy's portrait, found out what Mrs. Mason had to say concerning the artist. Now, however, the meeting waited; there was nothing for her to do but to plainly ask, if she wished her curiosity satisfied concerning Alida. She therefore told Mrs. Mason that she had been so charmed with Dorothy's portrait that she would like very much to have the same young lady paint a head of herself. Mrs. Mason was delighted at the success of her *protégée;* she would have liked to let the meeting go without a chairman and take Margaret herself to Alida's studio then and there; she finally persuaded Madame Fremiet to go by herself, and the two ladies got into Mrs. Mason's carriage, and Madame Fremiet was dropped at the big building where Alida had her studio.

I have often thought, concerning the picturesque and beautiful tale of Elaine dying for love of Sir Lancelot, that its mediæval setting alone rendered it

possible or probable. Towers were
probably damp, and the society and
amusements of mediæval women so
limited that there were few distrac-
tions. Young men too were not ex-
tremely plentiful; they were mostly
at the wars fighting the heathen. A
modern Elaine having met Sir Lancelot would have found, though he rode
away from his mother's house at seven
o'clock, that at eight she must get
ready to go to a dance or theatre
party. Then there would have been
the thousand-and-one duties and pleas-
ures which she absolutely could not
forego just for the sake of embroider-
ing a Kensington art square for his
shield. In the due course of time,
though she might never have thought
that any man was in any way equal
to Lancelot, she would probably, instead of dying in the most picturesque

manner and drifting down to Camelot, have married some one else, or at any rate engrossed herself in the many questions of the day and hour, so that her life, far from being ended with her one serious love affair, might rather be said to have been opened and ennobled by it. There be Lancelots and Elaines, but if Elaine has to work for her daily bread the universe will not feed her because Lancelot has ridden away.

Alida had been trying to work all day long, but there was no sitting up on top of the big ladder and singing as she had done the day before. She was physically numb and weary, and sat on a little stool in a heap close to the floor doing a conventional design across the bottom of the cartoon. Every now and then she would stop working and lean her aching head against the canvas. It would only be for a moment, then she would shake herself and go on. It would never do to break down.

Chloe was washing the kitchen floor and singing; the splash of the water and the old woman's droning, plaintive song grated on her nerves. The clock struck the hour slowly with its pretty, joyful French chime, the hour—just about the hour when Philip always came; but he would never come again. Her heart almost stopped beating with sick, faint dread, and hope as the bell rang as usual. Of course it must be some one else, yet she could not wait for Chloe; she answered the door herself, and there stood a tall, simply dressed lady, whose handsome face struck her as oddly familiar.

As Madame Fremiet in her most winning manner murmured explanations and her introduction through Mrs. Mason, she thought how strange it was that this little slip of a girl, with her large melancholy eyes and soulful face, should have come to be such a factor in her life. She doubted the truth of the anonymous letter at once; it was simply a calumny against herself, written, in spite of its uninterested avowal, simply to make mischief. She knew that Philip Herford was not a breaker of such small girls' hearts. She sat down in one of the carved chairs and talked to Alida with all the winning charm that she knew so well how to use, until the girl's shyness was quite overcome.

"May I ask," said Alida, "if I have the pleasure of speaking to Madame Fremiet whom I have seen play so often?"

Her face lit up as she spoke, and

Margaret realized what a charm lay in the flashing bright expression. The tone of the girl's unexpressed admiration went to her heart.

"Yes, I am Margaret Fremiet," she said, looking around the studio with evident interest. "Your portrait of Dorothy Mason is so charming I wondered if you'd do one of me."

A surprising change came over Alida; her languid, nerveless air disappeared, her pale face flushed, her eyes grew dark and humid; another young woman stood before Madame Fremiet—an artist to her finger tips.

"Do you really mean that you will sit to me for a portrait?" she cried. "It would be such an opportunity. I have seen you in every character you play. The first time I went to the theatre I saw you play Juliet—but perhaps it bores you to have me talk about your acting?"

"No, indeed," said Margaret. The girl's ardor touched a deep chord in her own essentially artistic nature. "One admirer, whose opinion I value, means more to me than columns of newspaper notices. So you saw me play Juliet. I shall never play Juliet again. I suppose it is a first warning that an actress gets that she is no longer young when she realizes that her Juliet is no longer as artistic as it was. You are fond of the theatre?"

"Oh, very. I have never known any one before who played."

Margaret leaned down comfortably in the soft embrace of the big chair. She was tired with her walk and Mrs. Mason's chatter; the studio seemed peaceful and quiet. She had come, she knew not why, in a somewhat theatrical mood which tickled her sense of humor, to find a RIVAL. She stayed with a sense of pleasure, talking to this big-eyed, enthusiastic child as though they had been old friends. She talked brilliantly of the stage and the drama, of people she knew, while Alida listened spellbound and enchanted.

"I shall not act much longer," she said at last. "To tell the truth, I am not well—all's not right here about my heart, as Hamlet says. The rest of my life, if there is going to be a rest of it, will have to be a quiet one. After my season closes here I shall only play once in a while for charity, as Nilsson does. But what about the portrait?"

"Could I do you in character as Imogen or Portia? No, I think I would rather do you just as you sit in that chair. Might I try some backgrounds?''

Margaret smiled at the girl's absorption in her art as Alida opened a big carved François I. chest and took out a great armful of draperies, the flotsam and jetsam of altar cloths and fair ladies' court gowns, silks, velvets, and rags that go to make up studio properties. One after another was pinned up on the wall behind the great carved chair, until at last a fine piece of Italian embroidery threw out all the beauty of Madame Fremiet's rich dark skin, and made her, even in her modish bonnet, a veritable queen.

Margaret had by this time worked herself into quite as great a state of enthusiasm regarding the portrait as though it had been a matter of long considered action and not the whim of a few hours. It was with great regret that she felt it would be impossible to give the sittings for the picture before her season closed, but these last weeks were being a terrible strain on her health, and she alone knew the hours of absolute rest that were necessary in order that she might appear herself for a few hours during the evening.

"You look tired," said Alida; "can't I give you a cup of tea?"

Margaret declined, rising hastily. The reason for her coming, which had been forgotten in the charm of the girl's presence, came into her mind again.

"I must be going," she said.

But Alida did not want her to go; her tone was so pressingly cordial that Madame Fremiet sat down again while the girl made the tea.

"I am very superstitious about the breaking of bread," said Alida. "I was so dull and lonely when you came in, and we have had such a charming afternoon, that I should like to have you drink a cup of tea with me for companionship."

"You are romantic," answered Margaret; "a bad quality in an unsentimental age. But you have such a charmingly miscellaneous collection of utensils to make your tea with that I can't refuse you. I don't doubt artistic tea is very much better than the ordinary kind."

She drank her tea with a keen sense of the humor of her visit, and stayed for quite a while longer, with kindly tact winning the girl to talk of her studio and work.

Alida forgot for a little while the sad tangle events had made in her life as they talked of the Louvre and the National Gallery and the Velasquez portraits in Spain, the girl's fine imaginative sense of beauty quickening the elder woman's recollection; and as Margaret rose and went away she could not help feeling an intense interest and liking for this odd child with her dreamy eyes, who talked of Bennozzo Gozzoli and Leonardo as other girls do of fashions and admirers.

Alida sat in front of the fire on the little stool and thought of her new friend and the portrait—what a good portrait she meant it to be, that should, in the parlance of studio slang, "go thundering down the ages." It is always so: the portrait that is to be painted on the blank canvas, the poem that is to be written on the paper which is spotless as yet; and even though when completed it may not "thunder" any more than the work that went before it or that will come after, still certainly the feeling is a good one, and nothing was ever any the worse because the ideal aimed at was a little too high to be reached.

The studio was quite dark, and Alida felt her thoughts turning again to Philip. She lit the gas and busied herself around the room putting away her materials and cleaning her palette. Then she went to the tea table, taking up the cup out of which Madame Fremiet had drank her tea. It was a pretty Sèvres cup marked with the N of the first Napoleon. She turned it round and round as though it was a precious memento, then dipping it in a cup of warm water she dried it carefully with her handkerchief and placed it on a shelf of a little teak-wood cabinet.

"I suppose," she thought to herself, "that I've got to get used to living along every day and getting as much happiness and good out of each person and thing as I can, and be thankful. When I'm an old lady, and of course I shall live to be a very, very old lady, I shall show that cup to people and tell them that the celebrated Madame Fremiet drank tea out of it. I don't see quite why I take this so hard," she went on, sitting down by the fire and gazing into the hot ashes. "What a baby I am. All the life seems to have been taken out of me. I've had harder times than this, too; it isn't nearly as hard really as the time when Chloe was so sick in Paris and all the money was gone. I thought she would die and leave me alone—then there was that awful night when she was so delirious, when I'd had nothing to eat all day and a terrible storm came up and almost blew in the windows.   What a wild night it was.   How the wind blows," she said, suddenly noticing it for the first time.

The wind had risen with the setting sun, the skylight rattled and shook, and the wind whistled wildly around the corners of the high buildings. She crouched before the fire, leaning her face on her hands. Chloe came in noiselessly and set a little table in one corner of the studio with a dainty cloth and delicate china, laying the one place as carefully as for a dinner party. Alida did not raise her head. Then there came a clatter of high heels down the hall, a rustle of skirts, and, late as it was, Mrs. Beckington, rosy and merry, homeward bound after a long round of calls, came bustling into the room. Alida pushed up her hair from her forehead with a

pathetic gesture of brain fatigue, trying to bring her thoughts and her wan
face to a cordial greeting of her visitor. Her tired smile went to Mrs.
Beckington's heart.

"I was just going by," she chirped
in her high voice, "and I thought to
myself, there's Miss Craig up there
going to eat her little dinner all by
herself, and I'll just carry her home
with me. Come, dear, jump into another dress or bring it around to my
house and dress there. Dorothy
Mason and Mr. Ashley are coming to
dinner and we will have a gay party."

Alida did not feel that she would be
any very magnificent addition to a
gay party, but she was not of the type
of young woman to shut herself up
and nurse her miseries.

"I hope you won't expect me to be
very gay, will you?" she said. "I've

a bad headache;" and she ran upstairs to get her dress.

Mrs. Beckington was not a very profound soul, much given to thinking. If she had been she might have moralized a little on Alida's characteristically womanly remark, "I have a headache."

Those headaches! What they cover—physical pain, broken hearts, anguish of body and mind; and still women, in patient covering of their miseries, say, and the world believes them, "I have a headache."

CHAPTER V

In the evening Philip Herford went
around to the Beckingtons' house.
He had dined at the club, had talked
over the tariff and the city govern-
ment with a trio of friends, and was
surprised on looking at his watch to
find it still so early in the evening.
He was as much at home at his sister's
as in his own house, and on being told
that the family were still at dinner, he
went up to the library and waited for
them to come upstairs. He looked idly
over Lang's last book, which lay on
the table, but that clever gentleman's
minute defence of the Homeric lines
did not prove of absorbing interest; he

IT WAS A WOMAN'S LONG SUÈDE GLOVE. (P. 99.)

read a few pages, and then, as he laid
the volume down, his eyes were caught
by a small object that lay on the floor
at his feet. He picked it up; it was a
woman's long suède glove, a rather
small size, with a faint perfume about
it. He patted the fingers out smooth
on his large palm, and then laughingly
put it down on the table, thinking that
it was one of his careless little sister's.
What a sentiment hovers over mate-
less gloves; how many poets have written of them, how many lovers cher-
ished them as keepsakes! Philip
wondered if Mr. Beckington senti-
mentalized much over his wife's gloves
now that he paid for them. Homer
and the epic being after all the only
source of amusement within reach,
he picked the book up again and
was deep in it when his sister glided
noiselessly through the portieres and

startled him by sitting down on the arm of his chair.

"You dear boy," she said, hugging his head regardless of his ears and the smoothness of his hair, "I've left them at dinner just to see you alone for a moment and congratulate you. Clarence has told me. I am so glad!"

Philip, with an utter disregard of his sister's finery, drew her down on his knees and held her for a moment, his cheek pressed against hers, just as he used to do when she was a fat, spoiled baby and he was a big hobble-dehoy boy. When he spoke his voice was a little husky.

"How very magnificent you are to-night," patting her chiffon ruffles; "have you a dinner party?"

"Only Dorothy Mason and Mr. Ashley, and "—catching sight of the glove—"there's Miss Craig's glove.

Philip, I was up in Miss Craig's studio this afternoon and I brought her down to dinner. She was sitting by the fire and looked so miserable and blue that my heart just ached for her. I'm afraid she is in some trouble; she has always been so bright and gay before. I wish I knew her well enough to ask her confidence, but I don't— do you?"

"No," said Philip. He looked down at the floor. He had not expected to meet Alida, had not wished to meet her so soon after their sad parting of the day before. "We all treat you like a baby, Bertha, you are so soft-hearted," he said; "we only have to give you a hint, and without asking why or wherefore you do just the right thing."

"Clarence said he wanted me to be nice to her. It's very sweet of you to say I do the right thing. I often think that I blunder around like a beetle; you see I just do things without very much reason. Clarence laughs at me so; he says that I haven't a bit of analytical mind."

" No, dear, you haven't, and I am glad of it. Deliver me from a woman with an analytical mind. Now, if I am going to stay this evening, I want you to tell Miss Craig very quietly before she comes upstairs that I am here."

The brother and sister looked into each other's eyes, eyes that were such a reflection of each other. Bertha got up off his knee, straightened her ruffles, puffed up her gauze sleeves, to all appearance a vision of beauty intent on rectifying the damages of a bear's hug. There were bits of character and sympathy in her nature, however, that were always cropping up, even to the astonishment of those who knew her best. She had almost left the room when she came back and laid her hand lightly on Philip's head.

"I do not want you to tell me anything," she said, with a little tremble in her voice. "You don't need to. You are all the brother I've got, and I can't help saying that I am sorry, oh, so sorry, for you and her."

She had flitted away before Philip could answer.

"I am so sorry too," thought Philip.

He did not return to reading his book. He had thought of Alida—how could he help it? He had known that she was suffering, trying to bear up bravely, but the certain knowledge of it gave him that sense of inability to deal with the circumstances that he had raised which often strikes one when the little breeze that one has fanned becomes a whirlwind. He pressed the little glove that he knew was hers to his lips. In all his life of luxury and wealth of all things that satisfy the soul and mind, he had never longed to possess anything quite as much as that little glove. He kissed it again and again.

"No, I have no right to you, little glove," he thought. "You have been worn before; your first finger is rough and soon you will be worn out and thrown away, but I shall never have the right to replace you. Go, little glove," he said, "and when she draws you up on her soft arm, teach her to forget one who is unworthy to kiss her shoe." He laid the glove on the table and picked up the book again, envying the worn piece of kid that had the right to go home with Alida and lie in a fragrant-scented drawer in her little white room. His reveries were soon interrupted again by a swishing of skirts and a sound of voices. Dinner was over. As they mounted the stairs he could hear Alida's voice, somewhat higher and more strained than she usually spoke, tossing witty replies back to Mr. Beckington.

They all came into the library, filling it with mirth and chatter. Philip shook hands with Dorothy and then with Alida, who was more self-possessed than he would have believed; her face was colorless and her eyes hard and bright with excitement, but she kept a good hold of herself and her pulse did not beat one bit faster for the meeting. In truth, Alida was more happy than troubled over his being there. There is a love so great that it casts out all jealousy, and that love was hers. She was so used to sorrow that one more deprivation, one more hardship, was simply just one thing more, the natural outcome of the fate that had pursued her from her birth. To snatch a few hours' happiness to see Philip with her own eyes, to be in the same room with him, was enough for her starved heart. She shook hands with him as coolly as with any other friend, and then with perfect composure turned to Mr. Beckington and went on talking.

"It's so nice of you to think I am original," she said; "you are very good about it, but some people seem to think me a new kind of animal whose habits and customs are to be studied like Mr. Crowley's; they never seem to realize that I have lived so long in studios and among artists that anything different seems original to me. The idea of living in a whole house strikes me as positively odd."

"You wouldn't find it odd, my dear," chirped Mrs. Beckington. "You'd find it a perfect bore if you had to look after a house. I'd like to live as you do, housekeeping is such a care."

"Yes, poor Bertha," said her husband, patting her plump shoulder, "she's a wreck from her household cares. But where do you suppose Gordon White is? He was to have dined with us, and he didn't come or send any word. We are really very much worried about him, for you know how punctilious he is."

Philip had not seen Mr. White at the club. In a person of his well-known regularity of habit his non-appearance at a dinner was indeed to be considered serious.

"I'm afraid he went to buy that doll for you, Bertha," said her brother, seeing that they were really anxious about their old friend. "He's probably got lost, and Clarence will have to advertise for him. 'A middle-aged bachelor, answering to the name of either Gordon or White, went to buy a doll for Mrs. Beckington; hasn't been heard of since.' That will sound finely in the *Evening Moon*, won't it?"

"I wouldn't be such a tease if I were you; probably he is sick or something, and you'll be sorry for having made fun of him. I think Mr. White is just the nicest man in the world and I won't have fun poked at him."

A smile rippled over her face as she

turned and beheld Gordon White, who was just entering the room. His appearance was, to say the least of it, so unlike that gentleman's usually collected demeanor that it was indeed calculated to raise mirth. In place of his quiet, self-contained air he seemed in a whirl of excitement. He had forgotten to remove his hat, which was pushed back on his head; his necktie was quite off the correct angle, and he was carrying an enormous brown paper parcel, evidently a large doll upside down, for two small feet in white socks and bronze shoes stuck pathetically out of the paper.

"Where have you been?" they all cried, laughing.

Mr. White did not seem to notice the amusement he caused. He went straight to Mrs. Beckington and laid the big package in her lap.

"It's the doll I got for you," he said, smiling, "and there are a few more things in the cab."

Dorothy and Alida knelt down by her chair as Bertha unwrapped the package and disclosed a lovely French doll dressed in long clothes. The women's enthusiasm over its beauties warmed Gordon White's withered heart. Certainly he was the hero of the hour for once, and he enjoyed it. He felt himself the good angel of the Christmas tree, and that he had never before fully realized what a happy time the holidays were.

"I got it at Macy's," he said, excitedly. "Did you ever go to Macy's? I asked the waiter at the club where to buy a doll, and he said Macy's, so I went there. It was just like the Stock Exchange, only women. There were so many dolls it was hard work deciding, but I thought this was a very nice one. Its eyes open and shut, and the young person assured me that its clothes come off. It's got a good cry, too.''

Mrs. Beckington squeaked the doll's cry in great glee. She really wished that she was a little girl again, that she might take off all its clothes and dress it. The men looked on at the pretty picture of the three women, and felt out of it in some way, and thought what funny, childish creatures women were, with a certain regretfulness that they were not the purchasers of the doll.

Meanwhile the footman had been bringing up from the cab a heterogeneous collection of toys. There was a Noah's ark, a tin kitchen, toys, puzzles, and games. Mr. White beamed; he had not been so actively happy for many days. The drive down lower Sixth Avenue, with its enormous white signs of cheap goods for sale, the interest of the curious, crowded store, and the amusement of choosing the toys, had warmed him into quite a Santa Claus glow.

"I bought a tin kitchen," he went on. "The young person said, 'Wouldn't you like a tin kitchen? They are greatly reduced; only sixty-seven cents; such a bargain!' I never got anything at a bargain in my life, so I thought I'd get the tin kitchen. I suppose now so many girls go to college there isn't such a demand for kitchens as there used to be," he said wisely.

"Just think of inculcating domesticity in some little girl," said Philip, picking up the toy, "by giving her a tin kitchen at a cost of sixty-seven cents. I know what I shall give you for Christmas, Dorothy, only I suppose you'd like to have one made of silver.

"No, I wouldn't. Do let me take it," said Dorothy. She was as anxious to play with it as a little girl. She took the kitchen to a distant corner of the room and set it on a table, where she was soon joined by Mr. Ashley.

"May I play with it too?" he said.

He had been watching her with some amusement, but when he spoke his face was quite grave and full of interest. He filled the little kettle with water from a carafe, and they were soon as absorbed as two children. Mrs. Beckington put down the doll and began examining the other playthings. The big Noah's ark interested her immensely. Her husband joined her, and they unwrapped the figures, setting them up in a row along the table.

I often think that a novelist who in a roomful of people describes the meeting of the hero and heroine would more nearly report the truth if he would place himself in the position of listener, catching the bits of talk that reach his ears. For that is life. Alida may have been breaking her heart, and she and Philip may meet with trembling souls; they may catch a moment and whisper a word to each other, but at the same time the chatter of others with gay hearts and peaceful souls will go on about them just the same. The hand-organs play out in the street although all within the house are mourning their dead.

Dorothy and Jim were playing with the kitchen, the Beckingtons were busy with the Noah's ark, and Mr. White was holding the doll, secretly consumed with a longing to see if its clothes really did come off. Alida sat watching them, and Philip came and sat beside her. For all the brightness of her eyes, he noticed how drawn her face was, and how tired. He had intended to say some commonplace, but instead he could not keep himself from saying:

"I did not know you were here when I came."

"It's just as well," she answered quickly. "I am glad that you stayed." She leaned back in her chair with absolute physical comfort to be near him and hear his voice.

"Do you suppose that is Shem or Ham?" cried Mrs. Beckington, holding up a small, straight, red figure. "I want to be sure, so as to have him

in the right place in the proces-
sion."

" What an excellent Sunday-school
scholar you must have been to remember their names, dear. Do you remember their wives' names too?"

Philip bent down his head close to
Alida's.

" Make a friend of Bertha," he said
in a low voice. " My hands are tied;
though you are in need, though you
are dying, I may not stir to help you.
Bertha is the sweetest soul alive, and
if you are friends it will make me feel
easier."

" Do you think that is a dicky bird
or a chicken?" said Mr. Beckington,
unwrapping a nondescript yellow
biped.

" I don't know," answered his wife
reflectively. " It looks to me like a
lizard, only it's got but two legs.

Here's a pine tree," she cried triumphantly. "I wonder why they had pine trees in the ark?"

"For Christmas trees, of course," answered Mr. White from his corner.

"I would like you to think kindly of one of us," Philip went on bitterly.

"Think kindly of you!" said Alida. "I always shall." She raised her clear dark eyes and looked straight into his face with fearless strength. "I have missed you so much," she said. "I can't help it, but I suppose I shall get used to it. Some time when I'm a little old lady still painting away in my studio, and you're an old, old man, you will come and see me again, won't you?"

"Jim isn't a bit nice," called out Dorothy from her corner. "He won't let me have his cigarette papers to burn in the range. Oh, do make

him give them to me, Mrs. Beckington!"

"Do you remember the day I was
doing that tapestry design," went on
Alida, "when you read me Arnold's
'Tristran and Iseult'? I often think
of it now how they sat together after
their restless, burning lives,

> "'Telling tales of separated lovers
> Reunited at their end at last.'

"It may be many years, but you
can think of me always at work and
always loving you."

"God bless you," murmured
Philip.

"What are you doing, Mr. White?"
cried Dorothy. Having burned up all
the cigarette papers, she was now
looking around for something new
to do.

The unlucky victim of her notice

had given way to his desire to undress the doll. Its little garments lay in a heap at his feet, and he was vainly struggling to get it back into a knit shirt. His embarrassment at finding the attention of the entire company riveted upon him was keen. He would have liked to strangle Dorothy. Mrs. Beckington flew to his rescue, and sitting down beside him, with deft fingers soon had clothed the doll suitably for an appearance in polite society.

The gayety began to jar on Alida, so she said good-night, and Mrs. Beckington, who saw that she was looking worn out, let her go without pressing.

She had been gone but a few moments when Madame Fremiet came in, as she often did for an hour after the theatre. If in the afternoon she was still a handsome woman, at night she was superb. Her eyes were dark and soft with the passion she had been simulating, and her whole presence breathed an intense magnetic attraction. She was followed by a man of about her own age, a tall, clean-cut Englishman with a reserved face and a gentle, kindly manner.

The Duke of Axminster was one of those Englishmen who do not come to America to get a rich wife. If he had ever given expression to any of his feelings, which he rarely did, he would have said that he considered Margaret Fremiet the finest woman in the world by all odds. As a younger man his one desire was to marry her, to the horror of his family, but when they found that under no circumstances would Margaret think of marrying him, they became almost as great victims of her charms as the

Duke himself. Years went by, and as Axminster did not marry, or take any notice of any other woman, for the matter of that, the marriage came to be the one desire of his mother's heart. Margaret's triumphal season the previous year in London had brought them closer together again, and when she returned to America the Duke did not delay long in following her.

Mrs. Beckington was enthusiastic in greeting her new guests. Nothing pleased her more than to have her friends drop in informally to late supper. The Duke, who admired Dorothy greatly as a most perfect specimen of the genus American bud, began a *tête-à-tête* with that lively young lady, to the terrible agony of her faithful lover.

Philip took a seat beside Madame

Fremiet. He wondered, in a vague way, seeing her in her rich, glorious beauty, fascinating, a queen of women, how his heart had gone out to the little brown bird perched in the high studio.

"What have you been playing to-night?" he said. "Ah, but I know—Portia. You have always something judicial in your mien afterward. I went to your hotel this afternoon, but you were away. May I come to-morrow?"

"Supper is served," said the butler.

And so we will leave them, a merry party going down to supper.

CHAPTER VI

The following afternoon Philip
Herford went to Madame Fremiet's.
As he waited in the flower-scented
parlor, filled with the many exquisite things that she always settled
around herself during her "encamp-
ments" for any length of time, the
subtle exotic charm that seemed to
breathe from her and from all her
belongings stole over his senses.
When at last Margaret entered the
room he was in a brown study, from
which he started as she laid her hand
on his shoulder.

"Ah, dear," he said, rising and
kissing her hand. "Your room is so

warm and fragrant that after the cold air it lulled my thoughts into sybaritic repose."

"What were you thinking of?" She settled herself into a comfortable corner of the sofa beside him, and looked up under her dark lids.

"I was thinking about—Margaret, do you know you are not looking well? Last night you were so gorgeously radiant; are you not well to-day?"

"How unkind of you, Philip—you suggest that I am no longer pretty in daylight. Of course I am all right."

She had been battling for hours with a bad attack of heart trouble, to which she was becoming more and more a victim. But she was terribly sensitive about this weakness; her glorious, robust health had been so long her great pride that she hated to confess herself an invalid. There had always been in her a sort of pagan pride of health and beauty—she could never grow old or be sick. She was looking pale to-day, which surprised Philip, who from one chance or another had never seen her after one of her bad attacks.

"You have big purple hollows under your eyes, my dear; why don't you confide in me if you are not well?"

"I'm all right; don't tease. Probably I did not get all the make-up off my face last evening, which accounts for my looks and your sympathy. Tell me, what have you been doing to-day?"

"Nothing. I've been to a book auction, but I want to talk to you seriously about something."

"Don't talk seriously," said Margaret. She was beginning to feel better and the reaction was setting in. The color came up into her face, and as she curled up in her corner she looked like a radiant beauty of twenty-five. " Don't let's be serious; let's play and talk nonsense. For all the years you have made love to me I've never known any one so delightfully and artistically flirtatious as you ; so ' woo me, woo me,' I'm in a humor to be won.''

Her dark eyes gleamed softly, her red, laughing mouth seemed a rose to be kissed, and in the languorous grace of her attitude she breathed a spell of enchantment. She wore a long, flowing tea-gown of rich purple silk, a curious Indian fabric shot with gold threads. It was such a gown that she had worn years before when Philip had called her in a poetic mood " my gold and purple butterfly." It had been his pet name for her ever since.

"My gold and purple butterfly," he said, leaning toward her, "I'm not in the mood to play at wooing, but to woo in earnest. I want you to let our engagement be announced at once; I want you to set a day, a very early one, dear, for our marriage."

Margaret looked at him keenly. His voice, every tone of which she knew by heart, rang as true as on the day when he had first told her that he loved her. Since her visit to Alida's studio Margaret had had time to think. What she had seen of the girl charmed her; she seemed such a slight, baby-ish little creature that she had laughed at herself for taking the least notice of the anonymous letter. Now as she looked into Philip's dark eyes she read there nothing but the natural desire of an ardent lover to consummate his marriage. She laughed softly.

"I want to wait until my engagement here is over. I couldn't stand the reporters and the newspapers. I've lived so long in the glare of publicity that I'm just like a romantic girl in this; I want it kept quiet. We have waited so long, six weeks isn't much longer; I cannot consent before. No, don't press me, Philip; I've waited so long that now on the brink of happiness I want to pause to play with fortune a little longer, and to come to you, when I do, not in a parade or show, but quietly and simply, as though I was still the young girl that I would I were; as though I had never seen the stage or known the love of any other man but you."

Philip kissed her cheek, and for a

few moments she was perfectly happy
and still in his embrace.

"It shall be just as you wish," he
said.   He had hoped that the engagement could be announced and the
marriage take place very soon, but he
realized all Margaret's objections.
He knew the trials of the publicity of
her position, and said no more.   For a
long time they sat in silence, then they
talked of the past, of their early days
together.   His *tête-à-tête* with Margaret was full of charm; every conversation seemed to disclose a new side
to her character.   She had entered
the room a grand, dignified creature in
her sweeping gown; in her confession
of her desire to keep their engagement
a secret, her face had worn the expression of a shy young girl; now she lay
back in her cushions a picture of sensuous and leonine beauty, talking with

regretful sentiment of the days that were no more.

"Shall I ever know you?" said Philip, struck by the changing of her manner, as in fact he often had been. "How little I know of you! Nothing would ever surprise me that you did or said, I see you under so many different guises. When we are married we won't settle down to not knowing what to say to each other in a hurry; you will have to tell me all about yourself, and it will be like Scheherezade's story: it will furnish me amusement and amazement for a thousand and one nights."

"It's because I am a Creole," said Margaret. "I think the races are divided into Caucasian, Mongolian—and Creole; but it's wonderful for all my exciting life how little there is to tell. You know that I married Monsieur Bonaventure when I was eighteen and that I was unhappy and miserable; that I suddenly became aware of my one talent and that I went on the stage." Her tone changed to a dreamy, reflective one. "I wonder if I did wrong? I had ties, duties, but I left them all, never thought of them. If it were to do over again I know I should do just as I did, and yet I regret—" She spoke with such sadness that Philip was touched.

"Don't regret what you did, dear," he said. "People with your genius are not to judge themselves by the narrow canons that are for the ordinary lot. It was your birthright to be an actress. Think how little the world is the loser by one good housewife less, how much it would have lost in not having your interpretations of Shakespeare."

"I know, but—" Margaret sat upright on the edge of the sofa, her parted lips showing her beautiful glistening teeth as though she was going to speak; then she lay back again among the pillows.

"What was it going to be, Margaret?"

"Nothing; I have changed my mind. Don't let's talk seriously any more; it makes me chilly—talking of my past sins always makes me want to commit a new set to blot out the old ones. Are you coming to see me act to-night?"

They talked a little longer, and then Philip went away, going down into the cold, chill street with crowding sensations of Margaret's beauty and charm, and cursing his own weakness and folly and the tangle he had made of others' lives.

Margaret lay quite still among the cushions for a long time, thinking of Philip and the years of their long waiting. Her life had been so good, so happy in its triumphs, in its joyous inner life. The room grew dark, and her maid came in and lighted the gas. She was a middle-aged Englishwoman devoted to her mistress.

"A caller, madame," she said softly, fearing that Margaret was asleep.

"Who is it, Barnes?"

"The Duke of Axminster." The woman could scarcely conceal her pride in a mistress who had a duke as a familiar caller.

Madame Fremiet straightened her hair, peeped into the glass to see that her dress was in order, and when the Duke entered was sitting before the fire, her tea table drawn up beside her—the majestic creature that the world knew and that Axminster never doubted was her real self. Margaret had stayed too much at Chilworth not to know just how the Duke took his tea; she made it now exactly to his taste.

The Duke, like many of his countrymen, was not an especially brilliant conversationalist; in fact, his qualities were largely national; but if he lacked the superficial graces, he certainly had most fully developed the dogged faithfulness and devotion for which Englishmen are noted. When he had drunk his tea and had read Margaret most of the contents of his mother's last letter, he unburdened his mind of a rumor that he had heard at the club —that Margaret was going to leave the stage and marry Philip Herford.

There is no such thing as breaking

unpleasant news gently. Margaret could say no more and no less than that it was true. She dwelt on her great friendship for the duke, her admiration for his mother, their untold kindness to her, but under all her gentle speeches the fact remained that she was going to marry Mr. Philip Herford as soon as her New York engagement was finished. She was surprised to see the effect that her words had. Ordinarily reserved and phlegmatic, the duke's self-possession was forgotten entirely; he paced the room with long strides, muttering to himself in his absorption.

"Do listen to me," said Margaret. "You would not have me pretend to care for you and marry you for your position, would you? Forget about me; your title and position make you, after the princes, one of the greatest

men in England. To me you will
always be one of the greatest and best
men I have ever known. Even if my
heart were not elsewhere, respect is
not love. You will marry some great
lady and be happy."

"My brother Dolworth is as sure of
the title as though I were dead," he
said. "You know there was only one
duchess for me, and I shall go back to
Chilworth and see her moving around
the rooms again as you did last summer,—as I would if you had really
been my wife, and died."

She had known Axminster for years;
his deep sentiment and feelings were
not unknown to her. There was something in his words that touched her
deeply. A sob rose in her throat.

"Years ago when you first refused
me I was almost mad with jealousy,"
he went on. "I have comforted my-

self all these years thinking that you did not care for me in the prime of your success and beauty, but that I would wait, and some time you would come to me when everything else was gone, when you were ill and alone. I have watched you lately; I know the effort it takes for you to keep up appearances—you are ill—I had hoped that you would come to me now. My shoulders are broad enough for you to rest your tired head upon, my heart is wide enough to be filled with happiness if it could be devoted to you."

Margaret dropped into a chair, sobbing.

"You are the best, the dearest friend ; but don't you understand, Duke, I love Mr. Herford ? Forget me, and give the duchess a more worthy daughter than I could ever be."

"Never!" His face was set with anger. "How little you know me! Since I have known you I have never seen any woman that could charm me for a moment. Yes, I have, though "—he stopped. "There was such a queer circumstance. I was going along in the dusk the other night when a woman passed me who I thought was you. I followed her; she was smaller, slighter than you are, a mere girl, but she made my pulses beat she was so like. She walked fast, and I followed her until she disappeared. Isn't it absurd—a man of my age chasing a little Bohemian because she reminded me of you?"

As he spoke a strange chill crept over Margaret, her eyes dilated, and she looked wildly and fixedly at him. Her face was gray and wan; she tried to speak, but her voice failed. He seized a carafe of water and gave her some to drink. She looked at him with pathetic eyes.

"Wait," she said; and then for a few moments he watched her fight for breath, and cold drops of perspiration stood out on his forehead in agony at seeing her suffer.

"Shall I call Barnes?"

"No; wait, just a moment."

She could scarcely speak above a whisper, and he knelt down beside her chair to catch her words.

"I'm not very well, I have these spells sometimes," she gasped. "As you were speaking a strange sensation of trouble and fear came over me. I have had such a warning before and it presages some trouble." The still, blank look came into her eyes again; she seemed almost in a trance. "You have waited so long for me, wait a

little longer.   I see trouble ahead.
Go now,'' she said hoarsely, '' but
come to-morrow.   I do not need you
to-night, but I may need you to-
morrow.''

At his sharp ring Barnes came hur-
rying in all devotion to her mistress.

That night, for the first time in all
her theatrical career, notice was sent
to close the theatre.   Owing to sudden illness Madame Fremiet did not
play that night.

"Girls," said Jenny Brady, dashing into her dressing-room about fifteen minutes before the curtain went up on "The Fencing Master"—"girls, you behold in me the 'duxit machina.'" She was in a terrible hurry; her hair was dropping down in disorder and her hat was on sideways.

"You'd better get dressed," said Augusta, commonly known as Gussy, Henderson, severely, who was dressed and sat polishing her nails in exasperating idleness, offering no assistance as Jenny tore off her clothes with a catching of hooks and tangling of laces.

"Wait till I get my wig on and then I'll help you, Jenny," said the third occupant of the room, who was small and thin and black and made up into a strawberry blonde. "Tell us what you've been up to."

"Do you remember when I was travelling with Shakespeare," said Jenny, unfastening the buttons of her boots with great energy, "and how Mr. Albert, the stage manager, told me Roman vestals weren't allowed to make eyes at the audience and docked my salary?" She daubed on her grease paint with a knowing hand. "I just swore that I'd be square with him, and so I am, all unbeknownst. He's managing Margaret Fremiet still at the —— Theatre. Yesterday I sent her an anonymous letter and to-night the theatre's shut up."

"A nice girl you are," said Gussy

scornfully, still polishing her nails, "breaking up the stars of the profession with your anonymous letters. Suppose your letter kills Margaret Fremiet, who's going to step into her shoes?"

"The letter wasn't killing," said Jenny contritely. "It only just told her the facts of Mr. Herford's devotion to my Miss Craig—if you hadn't been away over Sunday you'd have read it yourself. Gertie and me saw the letter in a novel what we'd been reading and just changed the names. You didn't catch cold up in Cornwall, did you, Gussy?" she went on plaintively. "Because, if you are not coming down with inflammation of the lungs again, I think you're pretty cantankerous."

"I'm not cantankerous," retorted Gussy, "but up in Cornwall I heard something awful—I heard that you posed for the 'nood.'" The scorn of her voice as she brought out the last word was indescribable. "We've got along very well as friends one way or another, we ain't any of us squeamish, but I draw the line at noods."

The strawberry blonde, her toilet completed, had laced up Jenny's bodice with quick fingers, and in a kindly way pulled up a wrinkle in her friend's tights.

"Jenny would be a good nood," she said reflectively.

The crimson blood flushed all over Jenny's face and arms and neck; she was so angry that she could not speak; she wanted to strike Gussy, but she knew that quarrelling in the dressing-room was absolutely forbidden.

"There's a nood in a picture gallery with a face just like yours," went on her tormentor. "A man painted it, a man named Hitchcock; and my friends up in Cornwall said it's just the living image of you."

"You ought to know me better, Gussy," said Jenny, controlling her tears, which she knew would spoil her make-up. "I've been posing for angels for Miss Craig and for a madonna for Mr. Hitchcock, and if he's seen fit to put my head on another woman's body I don't see what I can do about it. There ain't no harm in the nood anyway, Miss Craig says; but I ain't posed even for her—no, never!"

It was strange the affronted dignity that swelled the girl's person as she stood in the middle of the dingy room clad in her short dancing dress, which revealed an amplitude of limb, broad, beautiful shoulders, and white arms.

Her tone carried conviction to her listeners.

"Ain't my style, anyway," she said. "You girls wouldn't believe it if you was to see me standing up with my seraphim expression on. There are plenty of noods but there ain't many angels. I'd be a fool to cheapen myself. There's the call, girls." And they dashed up-stairs, and in a few minutes were mixed in with a bevy of similarly clad damsels treading the mazes of the amazons' march.

Readers that object to low life and low people I hope will excuse me for introducing them to not only one, but three such decidedly low characters as chorus girls. After all, we may not go on the street but we brush our skirts against those not conversant with all the exquisite subtleness of good and bad form. It is true they do not sit at our tables and their names are not on our visiting lists, but yet in the curious intertwining of our lives it is not outside the bounds of possibility that Jenny Brady, a chorus girl, should be bound up in the life of Philip Herford.

Days went by, long, busy days for Alida. Beyond a certain degree romanticism is only compatible with a settled income. Stained-glass firms would not wait nor spring exhibitions delay while Alida allowed her feelings to absorb her time. She settled herself to work, and in it found, as ever, the palliative for the woes of her mind. In her life, which had been absolutely starved of all affection, her little glimpse of love went a long way. Of passion she knew nothing; it is not fostered by untiring application to the study of the beautiful and working for bread. Not that her nature entirely lacked the elements of passion —no; but as yet she was in dreamland among her books and pictures. She had not as yet learned the mortal pain of love unfulfilled; her gray eyes looked out into the world with the innocence of a child. She had never been used to such companionship of her own age before, her work had been too absorbing to give much time to play; but now that her reputation was won and the hard bread-struggle over, she could afford to allow herself a little freedom.

Mrs. Beckington and Dorothy were always running in on some perfectly charming errand or other. Would she go for a drive? Or would she go to the opera that night? Or would she make them some tea and advise them about a dress? It was a gentle, aimless companionship and a chattering of the small nothings that go to make up the substance of fashionable women's lives. But Alida enjoyed it thoroughly. She little supposed that beside their constant kindness she had a third watchful angel in Jenny Brady. The girl's rough honesty always pleased Alida, and lately, as she stood on the platform posing for angels and madonnas, she would give vent to a torrent of quick Irish wit that would lighten Alida's mood unthinkingly.

Chloe working in the kitchen became quite jealous of the peals of girlish laughter that would resound from the studio during work hours. The truth was that Jenny, finding that her anonymous letter had not had the least effect on straightening out Alida's life, laid Philip down very deep in her

" villain " list, and all her heart went out in the active, everyday missionary work of trying to make Alida laugh.

"May I stop at four sharp?" she said one afternoon. "I'm going to my friend Miss O'Halloran's reception this afternoon, and we have to keep early hours so as not to be late for the theatre."

Alida knew all about the three friends, how they shared the same dressing-room at the theatre, how they lent each other money when times were hard, and nursed each other when they were ill. She knew all of Jenny's life, or at least all that could be told of her experiences. Through her advice Jenny, settled in New York for one winter, had taken a tiny flat in Harlem with her two friends. Regarding this little tea, at which, with all the airs Dorothy

Mason could have assumed, Jenny was to preside, she had heard much during the last few days, enjoying thoroughly Jenny's attempts at domesticity, and taking great pleasure in telling her of the latest things she had seen at teas she had been to.

"You'd better go now, Jenny, I'm pretty tired," she said a few minutes before four, and the girl shuffled off in her sandals.

"Angels must have a queer gait if they wear them things," she said to herself, twisting up her auburn locks and divesting herself of her flowing robes. "When shall I come again?" she called, with her mouth full of pins. "I've got to go to Mr. Hitchcock's to-morrow."

"Day after," said Alida, "and I'll be sure to finish the cartoon then. I don't know what I should do without you, Jenny; you work right into my ways; some models make me so nervous.''

'' Oh, you're easy to pose for; nothing like some of them, that won't let you wink, and pin folds right through your skin. The only thing that's hard work about angels is keeping your eyes rolled up to heaven; it gives you a crick in the back of your neck. But then there's always something—and it's nothing to having to stand with your mouth open. I won't pose for any more singers. There's the bell! Now, I suppose that's Mrs. Beckington or Mrs. Mason,'' she thought, secretly rather jealous of the interest they took in Alida.

It was Dorothy, fresh and sweet as a rose, her pink and white complexion set off charmingly by a faultless costume of tobacco brown and a broad

SHE HELD BY A LEASH A BIG ST. BERNARD. (P. 153.)

brown hat with big plumes. She
held by a leash a big St. Bernard,
which added to her picturesque effect.

"I've been having such a good walk
with the bow-wow," she chattered,
"and I was so hungry I thought I'd
just come in and see if there wasn't
tea and perhaps muffins up here. I'm
just starved, and mamma would die if
I went anywhere alone to buy anything more filling than caramels."

Alida was very glad to see Dorothy.
She promised to treat her to unlimited
muffins.

"But, alas!" she said, glancing at
the girl's beautiful dress, "Chloe is
not well this afternoon and we shall
have to do them ourselves, and I am
afraid you are far too elegant for the
kitchen."

"Nonsense, lead the way," said
Dorothy stoutly. "If you knew the

pangs of hunger that I am suffering under this gorgeous garment, you wouldn't delay."

At this moment Jenny came down from the bedroom, quiet, and looking quite like a lady in her neat-fitting tailor gown.

"Good-by, I'll come Thursday," closing the door softly after her.

Her position as model was full of speculation to Dorothy's inquiring mind. She would have liked to talk to her, but Jenny was shy, and beyond the respectful "good afternoon" was never known to utter a word in her presence, for Jenny Brady had a very great weakness: she took much thought of her personal appearance and her clothes, and prided herself that men and women passing her on the street saw in the quiet elegance of her attire the possession of a fortune and a Fifth Avenue house. She oddly realized her limitations.

"I'm all very well as long as I keep my mouth shut," she would say, "but my brogue is a dead give-away."

Before groomed, fresh, well-trained Dorothy she felt herself an awkward sham and sank into a meekness worthy of an English housemaid.

The two girls went into the kitchen and began cutting up the muffins, when the door-bell rang violently with the peculiar ring that was usually followed by Mr. Ashley, come, through one reason or another, to call at just the opportune time when his lady love was there. These visits had rather disturbed Alida until she found that he had usually been to the house and that Mrs. Mason had sent him around.

The game of cross purposes is a gay

one. Dorothy was intent on concealing her engagement, Mr. Ashley was equally intent on having it announced, and Mrs. Mason, seeing in Mr. Ashley an excellent *parti*, like an amiable, worthy mother was moving heaven and earth and losing her midnight sleep inventing opportunities to throw them together.

Dorothy peeped out through the kitchen door, and when she saw who the visitor was, nothing would suit her but that her lover, in all the magnificence of his immaculate frock coat and fresh gloves, should come in and see the kitchen. Dorothy sat in front of the range toasting her muffins as though it were one of her daily duties. Alida was rather disturbed at her two magnificent guests insisting on occupying the little room.

"Dorothy is so spoiled," she said in

apology, "that if she wants you in the kitchen, you'll have to go; but really I don't think you'd better, it's such a little place and there is only one chair."

But Mr. Ashley would not hear of being treated as a stranger, and he insisted upon coming into the kitchen to see Dorothy in her latest, as a beautiful picture of domesticity. He scorned the chair, and would sit on top of the tubs, swinging his feet, a perfectly absurd picture in his immaculate attire, with a background of blue plates and copper kettles.

"Miss Mason," he remarked airily, "I hope you are getting a few points in housekeeping."

"I've been taking cooking lessons for two years," in great dignity, which was rather upset by finding that in her interest at his arrival she had forgotten to turn the toasting-fork and her muffin was a cinder.

Mr. Ashley took the fork from her hand and insisted upon toasting the muffins himself; with the handy fingers of a college boy used to making all kinds of messes in his room, toast-making was a fine art. Dorothy watched him, with a high degree of respect creeping into her mind as she contrasted his golden-brown circles with her cindery ones. Mr. Ashley and Alida had become warm friends during the past few weeks; he admired the plucky little artist with all the amazement of a man who was unused to see a lady work for her bread. He hoped that she would persuade Dorothy to have their engagement announced, but so far no persuasion could move that romantic young person.

When the muffins were toasted Mr. Ashley turned violently around in his chair, took a newspaper from his pocket, and looked sternly at Dorothy.

"What do you suppose I read in the *Town Tattler* to-day," he cried, his voice ringing with anger and indignation as he read the obnoxious paragraph. "'Miss Dorothy Mason is, we are told, the fortunate young lady whom the Duke of Axminster will bear away to Chilworth Castle.' Oh, Dorothy," he said, rumpling up his thick hair, that he had spent goodness knows how long reducing to a perfect polish, "I can't stand your being spoken of publicly in this way. I feel crazy, quite crazy; I didn't sleep a wink last night." In his agitation he waved the toasting-fork wildly around.

Dorothy's teasing nature was highly

pleased; the more her faithful lover fumed the more light-hearted she got.

" Of course the Duke has paid me a great deal of attention," she said mockingly.

Mr. Ashley's honest eyes flashed indignantly.

" He'd no right to pay you attention. You should be ashamed of yourself, an engaged girl. It's all great fun for you, I suppose, but a man can't stand it. I'm haunted at night thinking you are dancing with some other man; I can't eat my dinner thinking of you sitting at the other end of the table smiling at—"

" Some other idiot," retorted Dorothy calmly.

Her enraged lover glared at her fiercely. The bell rang again, and Alida slipped from the room, hoping that they would come to some kind of an understanding.

"I'm going straight down to the *Town Tattler* office," he said, getting up out of the chair, his big figure seeming to fill the entire room, "and I'm going to say to them, You've got to contradict that report; she's engaged to me—me—me—and I was captain of the football team at Yale."

He looked so funny and determined that Dorothy could scarcely keep from laughing. At the same time her *amour propre* was pleased by the evident earnestness of his affection for her.

"Oh, Jim, how much you do love me," she said, suppressing a giggle.

"Do I?" said Mr. Ashley, sarcastically. "Do I indeed?" His face was hard and determined. Like many another patient soul, when his amiability had come to an end, he was perfectly remorseless. "No, Dorothy Mason, I don't love you." And as Dorothy, taken by surprise, put up her pretty red lips to be kissed, he seized her by the arm in anything but a gentle grip. "Kiss you! Indeed I won't," he said, with withering scorn. "I'm not in the habit of kissing young ladies to whom I'm not engaged. Come along to the studio; it's most improper our being here without a chaperon."

Dorothy was so surprised she couldn't speak; she picked up the plate of muffins with lamblike meekness and followed her irate lover into the studio.

Alida was standing in the centre of the room, looking startled and perturbed, while not far from her a somewhat flashily dressed young man was talking rapidly in rather loud tones. "This is the most extraordinary thing," cried Alida, turning to Jim. "I don't exactly understand it, but this gentleman and a newspaper and Jenny Brady seem very much mixed up." The man turned, instantly including Jim in the conversation.

"There's an article about Miss Craig just been set up at the *Evening Budget*, where I'm employed—oh, I'm not a member of the staff, I don't mean that," he went on frankly, "but we manage to know a good deal that goes on. I was walking uptown just now with a particular lady friend of mine, Miss Jenny Brady, and I told her about it. She blazed right up and said, 'Miss Craig would object to it, and she'd never speak to me again if I didn't try to stop its being published.' So I thought the best thing I could do was to come and ask Miss Craig about it myself."

"Well, I don't care for newspaper articles much," said Alida, "but as long as I exhibit my work publicly I don't quite see why I should object to its being noticed."

"The public don't care much for pictures, begging your pardon," said Mr. Blair. "But 'tis reported that you are engaged to Mr. Philip Herford; that's what brought the matter up."

Poor Alida; her face went ashy and wan. That her secret must be dragged forth into public criticism to furnish a newspaper item seemed the very last straw.

"Not that it's anything to have your engagement anounced when it's not true," said Mr. Blair, with rough kindness. "Lots of young ladies—"

But Jim, broad of shoulder and thick of head, realized what the girl was suffering.

"Mr. Blair," he said, "I don't think Miss Craig or her friends can ever thank you enough for coming and letting us know of this. I think, perhaps, I can prevent the article being published; my father owns some stock in the *Evening Budget*, and one of my cousins is on the staff— Tom Ashley, perhaps you know him?"

"Oh, yes; he's the sporting editor. I guess he could fix it for you."

"Thank you very much, Mr. Blair," said Alida, putting out her hand as the young man, his errand now accomplished, was making for the door.

Mr. Blair shook it with a hearty grip. "You won't let on 'twas me?" he said knowingly to Jim.

"No, indeed, and thank you for coming."

"Wasn't it good of him?" cried Dorothy, when the door closed. "I just hope he will get to be a reporter and an editor and everything else that is fine."

"Do you really think you can stop the article?" said Alida breathlessly. Despite Jim's comforting assurance she connected the making of a paper with things unalterable, like the solar system and gravitation. Jim's kindly heart held an immense amount of consideration for all feminine creatures. Alida in distress appealed to every fibre of his being.

"I'll do the best I can, only "—he stammered, trying not to hurt her— "you must excuse my asking the question, but are you engaged to Mr. Herford or not?"

Alida simply shook her head in denial.

"Then I'm off; I'll tell them they can print anything they like about your pictures or studio, but nothing personal. Now don't worry one bit. Tommy Ashley will fix the whole thing up for me in a jiffy; he's the best sort. Dorothy will stay with you until I come back."

"Oh, go, do, you dear, good, big boy," cried Alida, tears of relief springing to her eyes.

"Yes, go," cried Dorothy.

So without another word Mr. Ashley seized his coat and flung himself down the hall, while the girls stood looking after him, dazed with astonishment at the whole scene. An unfortunate love affair might have attractions for Dorothy's romantic mind in theory, but to know that in real life her dear friend was suffering was another matter. She knelt down beside Alida, wrapping her in her strong young arms, and for a few moments the two girls sobbed together, shedding tears of sympathy that brought relief to poor Alida's troubled heart.

CHAPTER VIII

Philip was very much alarmed at
the news of the closing of the theatre.
He went immediately to the Plaza
Hotel, but Margaret could see no one.
Barnes met him in the little perfumed
sitting-room, and told him, with perfect frankness, the terrible condition
of health her mistress was in, and
that this attack was no worse than
many she had had. Barnes, who perfectly adored her mistress, yet had
little patience with the folly of a person who, to finish out a theatrical
engagement, would delay marrying
either a duke or a millionnaire, wished
that either of the men would insist on

marrying Madame Fremiet then and there. She exaggerated her mistress's condition with this object in view, and Philip went away troubled and torn with anxiety.

The Duke came in a few minutes later and Barnes went over the same scene with him. Being an English-woman, she naturally felt that a woman who might be a duchess, and wouldn't, was flying in the face of Providence.

It was Sunday morning ; a warm, fresh, spring-like day, the sun sweep-ing over Fifth Avenue, blazoning the bonnets and gowns of pretty women on their way to church. As Philip went along he bowed continually to right and left; every one seemed abroad. Mrs. Beckington flitted by, and Dorothy and Mrs. Mason, carrying their prayer-books, to St. Thomas's.

At last he met an old college friend, "Tommy" Barlow, as he was still called by his contemporaries, though he was now junior member in the important law firm of Renwick, Rainsford & Barlow. It had been through this firm that the official announcement of her husband M. Bonaventure's death and of the disposition of his property had come to Madame Fremiet. With that wonderful insight that comes to lawyers and physicians, making their consciences strongboxes to hold the secrets of others' lives, Mr. Barlow had very quickly realized the intimate connection of his old friend with the celebrated actress. He was so charmed with the dignity that Margaret showed in absolutely repudiating any wish to share in her husband's estate or to derive any benefit from one who, in his lifetime, had never been anything to her but an influence for evil; that he admired Margaret as much for her womanly dignity as for the magnetic attraction which she had for all who came in contact with her.

Mr. Barlow was a notable pedestrian, and the two men soon struck out of the fashionable crowd, and keeping step as they had done in college marching, covered block after block, exploring the border-lands of the new parks and discussing appropriations, etc., as though their lives depended upon the solution of the city problems. Then they went back for lunch to Philip's house in Forty-seventh Street, where, after the manner of bachelor households, the meals were very much at the whim of the master. It was a beautiful house, full of rare and lovely things, and the dining-room where they sat was furnished with old carved Italian chairs from some Genoese palace, and rich hangings in shades of peacock, while a frieze of the sacred birds ran around the wall, painted by a famous artist's hand in a glory of gem-like color.

Mr. Barlow could not help thinking how well Madame Fremiet would fit into such a beautiful setting ; how she would look, with the regal poise of her head and her magnificent shoulders, seated in one of the great chairs at the head of the table. Philip was thinking the same thing too, as he had thought it so often since the night of his majority, when he had allowed no gayeties, no guests, but had sat alone in the beautiful room, with one other place set opposite his at the table, with a bunch of marguerites laid beside the plate. Then, when the butler had left the room, he had stood up and drank to Margaret, who was hundreds of miles away. Perhaps it was fantastic—well, youth may be forgiven for its fantasy; it passes quickly enough, and then there is no more poetry in the calm reason that experience has taught.

Philip's train of thought was interrupted as his eye caught the glint of a gold frame that hung in the picture gallery, opening out of the room where they sat—the frame that he knew so well, on Alida's little picture, which had been the cause of their meeting and friendship. For a moment he almost envied Mr. Barlow the recollection of a quiet grave up among the New England hills, where they had laid his sweetheart many years before. Whose loss had cut deep lines and thinned his hair long before his time, and made him the most confirmed of gentle bachelors.

"I've just had some new Elzevirs sent over from the Duc de Romarteau's sale at the Hôtel Drouot. Won't you come up to the library and see them?" he said.

It was a long day in spite of the Elzevirs. Philip had been cut to the heart by Barnes's description of her mistress's sufferings. He wanted to see Margaret, to assure her of his devotion, and he thanked heaven that he had not laid an extra burden of sorrow on her shoulders through any selfishness in his love for Alida. The concealment of her illness touched him infinitely. Brave Margaret, striving to keep up her queenly regalness. "God be merciful to me a sinner," he thought. He went up to the Plaza in the evening again, but the physician had absolutely forbidden Margaret seeing him; she sent out a little note by Barnes, playful and gay as ever.

"My Dear:

"I am better, but so lazy and tired. Don't worry about me. I shall be up to-morrow, and will be able to finish out my engagement.

"Good night.

"Margaret."

Philip went on to Mrs. Beckington's, for he knew she would be anxious to hear the latest report from the sick one. The house was crowded with guests, assembled for an informal Sunday night musicale. He was not in the mood to be gay or even decently civil to the beautifully gowned women who were scattered about in groups of exquisite color pictures. After whispering a few words to Bertha, he was going away, when she said:

" Don't go; Paderewski is going to play. Run up in the library, it will be perfectly quiet there. Stay, Philip, do; you look so white and ashy that I can't bear to have you go. I'll turn all the women out first."

He saw that her soft, sympathetic little heart was really troubled, and gladly went upstairs out of the chatter and din of high feminine voices, to the dim, cool library, where he dropped into a big leather chair, wearied in body and mind. The chatter of gay voices that reached his ears suddenly ceased; the big house was silent. Philip listened as the first tones of the melody began. Paderewski was playing, and after the disturbance of the past weeks the notes fell like balm on his sore spirit.

I am not going to devote much space to a description of the great pianist's art; only let any one whose soul is distraught and vexed with the cares of the world look back to the exquisite simplicity, the sincerity of nature, with which he interprets the Schubert melodies. They took Philip away to the healing influence of green woods, full of cool, gray, summer shadows, where the piping of little birds is the only sound and the light of lovers' eyes the only speech. He crouched in the corner, hiding even from the dim light. Then applause and a chatter of voices reached him, then quiet and the clear, joyous tones again. A cool breath seemed to be passing over his fevered soul; he was coming out into the calm after the storm and stress of the past weeks.

The library was a quaint place, lined with shelves and made into small alcoves by low book-cases, so that several people, in their nooks, might enjoy the privacy of their favorite volumes. When the music ceased, Philip sat crouched in his chair undisturbed for a long time, and was so absorbed in thought that he scarcely noticed the gentle swish of a skirt that passed him by, and settled itself in another alcove. The room was so still that the newcomers, evidently thinking that they were the only occupants, soon forgot to cautiously lower their voices. The couple were no other than Dorothy Mason and Mr. Ashley, who had stolen away after the music was over to snatch a moment's *tête-à-tête*. The *tête-à-tête*, however, having been snatched, did not seem to bring that unalloyed happiness with it that they had anticipated.

Dorothy was looking bewitchingly pretty, but she was also bewitchingly teasing. Lately she had been flirting, so wildly that Jim's heart was quite broken. He had come to Mrs. Beckington's firmly resolved to master his lady love, but his courage quite failed him at her sweet looks, and he would have put off his scolding until the morrow had not Dorothy, nestling like a glowing rose in the arms of the big leather chair, begun a series of pin-picking teasings. He answered her at random for some time, which only increased her naughtiness. Finally he arose and stood towering over her in an attitude of great dignity. Utterly ignoring the air of persiflage with which she had been treating him for the past half hour, he began a long, stammering monologue which finally conveyed to Dorothy's astonished mind the idea that she had been brought up to the library that Jim might break to her as gently as possible the fact that their engagement was at an end. He was so quiet and determined that Dorothy could only look at him with horror-stricken eyes. His face twitched nervously, an evidence to Dorothy of deep emotion; he was embarrassed, grieved, but evidently bent on separation.

"You see, Dorothy, you wouldn't have it announced," he stammered, "and I—" —it went to Jim's kindly heart to even make believe care for any other woman—"I'm—" He was unable to get any further, but took out of his pocket a copy of the *Town Tattler* and began to read from it: "Mr. Ashley, member of the Calumet, etc., is reported to be engaged to Miss Alma—"

He got no further. Dorothy sprang from her chair wildly and took hold of his arm; her voice rang through the ears of the occupant of the next alcove.

"You ought to be ashamed of yourself, Jim Ashley, flirting so when you know I love you with all my heart and soul! Oh—" and in a torrent of tears she threw her engagement ring at him and flew out of the room, a whirl of flowing tulle and ribbons.

Jim stood petrified. His carefully thought-out plan hadn't succeeded very well. There was a great lump in his throat as he picked up the ring, which he had bought with a great slice of his sophomore allowance, and which Dorothy had worn so faithfully ever since. Philip, roused by the girl's flight, thought it was about time he should make his presence known. He rose, and looked over the top of the dividing book-case, and there stood Jim gazing blankly at the little gold circlet that lay in his broad palm.

"May I ask, Jim," he said kindly, "what is the meaning of your corraling my sister's guests and scaring them into hysterics?"

Jim started at seeing the sudden apparition of Philip's face looking at him over the book-case. There was a moment's pause, and then he went around into the other alcove and talked about Dorothy. Jim had been a very little boy when Philip was a big one, and the younger man still looked up to the elder with the admiration, if not with the awe, of his childish days. He poured out his whole heart about his engagement and Dorothy's foolish, romantic notions. Jim was not particularly brilliant, but when he had an idea he had it strong. He confided to Philip that it had struck him after he had reproached Dorothy for the article that had appeared in the *Town Tattler*, announcing her engagement to the Duke of Axminster, that if such an article should appear about himself, it might make her jealous and bring her to terms. But, alas for his cleverly concocted plan, it had been carried out most disastrously. In their two years' engagement they had had many quarrels, but never one so serious as this, for Dorothy had returned him his ring. He held out the little circle pathetically to Philip, the poor little ring that had been so faithfully worn for two years. Philip listened sympathetically.

"If I were you," he said, "I shouldn't be the least bit discouraged. I'd go right downstairs now and find Dorothy; she's probably nearer giving in than she's ever been before. I'd run right along."

Jim went. He found Dorothy in her pretty evening cloak, ready to go home; the carriage was waiting for her, and she went swiftly downstairs past him, followed by her mother's middle-aged maid carrying her flowers and fan. Jim followed them out to the carriage; it was a clear moonlight night. He laid his hand masterfully on Dorothy's arm.

"Wait a moment," he said; then he helped the maid into the carriage. The Masons' house was only a few blocks away. "We are going to walk around," he said, with such an air of authority that the servant, who was, as all good servants are, highly interested in the affairs of the family, thought something must have happened.

Jim drew Dorothy's hand through his arm. Her face was tear-stained and gentle, and she looked bewitchingly pretty with her curls blowing in the wind, as they escaped from the lace fichu that was tied around her head.

We will leave them walking through the moonlit streets. Only half a dozen blocks, but what a difference it made! When they reached the Masons' house the engagement ring had mysteriously found its way again into Dorothy's possession, only this time it was on her finger.

"I'll come and see you to-morrow morning," said Jim, as the footman bustled down from the carriage to let

Dorothy in, as though she had come home quite as she should have.

He went down the street with long, rapid strides, down the street that was so different now that there was no Dorothy walking beside him, bunched up in her long cloak and making his steps slow and irregular as she pattered along in her fur boots. There are romances—yes, though we grow rich and well dressed and keep a carriage; aye, even in our nineteenth century, and our Dorothys and Mr. Ashleys still walk in the moonlight, and the maid whispers to the coach-man, and he drives the carriage around by the side street to meet them at the door, as though every-thing were quite regular.

When the last guest had gone and the last carriage rolled away—quite early, too, only twelve o'clock, for it is a law that Sunday entertainments are early—Mr. and Mrs. Beckington went up to their rooms for the night. Bertha's eyes were bright with excitement and the joy of the great pianist's music.   As she began unfastening her bodice, her husband, noticing the sweet expression that her face wore, bent down and kissed her reverently. He had been married too long to be surprised, or in fact to have it detract from his worshipful love of her, that her little rosebud mouth, upon returning his kiss, murmured sweetly:

"Oh, Clarence, I'm so hungry."

"Are you, dear? I'll go down and see if there isn't some supper left."

"No, I don't want salads and things ; I wish—oh—" she pursed up her mouth into the most delightful red button—"how I wish I had a pie!"

No wonder her husband adored Mrs. Beckington: she was the most delightful creature, she looked like a cunning cherub, was hungry and wanted pie.

"Go down and forage, that's a dear," she said coaxingly; "get something good, we can eat it up here. I don't doubt the servants have pies and all sorts of good things that we never have."

Thus urged, Mr. Beckington put on his coat and went downstairs, and Bertha slipped out of her dress and into a charming pink negligee. Early in the course of her married life this little fragile woman had utterly subdued her husband by the indigestible things that she could eat at midnight. Never a large eater, salads, patés and party suppers were nothing to her. She slept like a top after coffee; Welsh rabbits never made her turn in her sleep, and once she had confessed that her favorite midnight dish was hard-boiled eggs and crackers.

It always tickled Mr. Beckington's sense of humor to go prowling around with a candle in his own house, stealing eatables from his own butler's pantry. He returned to his wife with a bottle of champagne and a pie—a big, handsome mince pie. They set the tray on a little Louis Quinze table, and Mrs. Beckington ate her piece with such a relish that her example was quite infectious, and her husband could not forbear helping himself to one too. They had a good time together, these young married people, sitting in their cosey chairs drinking their champagne and talking over the evening and their friends; Mrs. Beckington, as a woman will, expecting her husband to take a deep interest in how well Miss R. looked, and what an ugly gown Mrs. J. had on, etc., for nothing passed unnoticed by her bright eyes, despite her duties as a hostess and her enjoyment of Paderewski's playing. The pie became quite a wreck of its former self during their talk, and it was nearly two o'clock before they thought that it was getting late, and Mr. Beckington rushed off to his dressing-room. At last Bertha laid her pretty head on her pillow, and before she dropped into the dreamless, childlike sleep that comes to those so healthy in mind and body, she thought how happy all her life was, how good her husband was, how much every one loved her. She had noticed, during the music, tears in Alida's eyes, which the girl tried to choke back. It seemed to Bertha as though her tears were different from the pearly tribute that so many of the other women shed in homage to the great pianist, and she had put out her hand and held Alida's under the cover of her tulle skirt.

"I hope poor little Alida will be happy some day too—as happy as I am," was her last thought as she fell asleep.

CHAPTER IX

Although the objectionable paragraph concerning Philip did not appear in the *Evening Budget*, the unpleasant circumstance did not pass quickly from Alida's mind. The article, illustrated by a badly drawn sketch of herself and one of her pictures, came out in the course of time, and a copy was sent to her. She read over the list of her charms and accomplishments with some amusement, wondering why people should care for such trivialities. Dorothy and Mrs. Beckington were quite pleased with the article, only they did not think that it praised her work quite enough. Jenny Brady loved it; she read it to all her friends and dilated upon it enthusiastically. One day she confided to Alida that a particular gentleman friend of hers had written it.

Alida never had the heart to tell her the annoyance of the interview; she was very glad of her forbearance, as Jenny's confidences concerning the "particular gentleman friend" grew more and more frequent, until she finally announced that she was going to be married—and to whom but Mr. Blair, the sturdy reporter of the *Evening Budget* with whom we have a slight acquaintance?

Let no one look askance at the mundane love of a chorus girl, eking out her pittance posing for angels, and a young man connected with the mysterious inner workings of the blurredly printed and unreliable *Evening Budget.* Probably no woman ever took a deeper interest than Jenny in the details of her modest trousseau, and surely there is a sentiment about wedding clothes, even though they be bought at bargain sales in cheap shops. As for the narrow Harlem house that they were having fitted up on the installment plan by an Eighth Avenue furnishing house, it was "home" to them, and they took a tremendous amount of pride in it; and though it was only a vulgar little place, with bright carpets and Nottingham lace curtains, I doubt, if judged from a really æsthetic standpoint—as, for instance, from the standard of even the lowest caste of Japanese—it would have been considered any worse taste than some of our wealthiest houses.

When Jenny's father from his downtown liquor saloon heard of his daughter's approaching marriage—he had not taken the slightest notice of her for years—he sent her word that he had heard of the great marriage that she was going to make with the literary gent, and that he was quite willing to give her a fine wedding, hire Minerva Hall and do everything in great style. Truth to tell, the real meaning of these magnificent overtures on the part of Jenny's father was to be laid to the fact that his rival, on the opposite corner of Hester Street, had just married off his only daughter in great style, with the ceremony in the cathedral, and a wedding breakfast which had been attended by four or five hundred people, as had been duly reported in the papers the following day.

There had been the severest rivalry between the opposition shops for many years. Mr. Brady never felt that he had been gotten the better of until the wedding. He could scarcely be married himself, having a middle-aged and devoted wife, but he really thought of hunting up his daughter and seeing if she wouldn't marry somebody to put the nose of "that Donovan" out of joint. Maggie Donovan had only married the bartender in her father's saloon, and when Mr. Brady heard of Jenny's approaching marriage to Mr. Blair his paternal bosom swelled with pride.

But Jenny was not to be tempted by a list of the magnificent presents that the politicians had sent to Maggie Donovan, nor by the vast quantities of champagne that Mr. Brady guaranteed should flow.   She had not associated so long with Alida without gaining some elements of refinement.

"I'm going to be married like a lady," was all she said in reply to her father.

And so she was, quietly one morning in church, in a gray travelling dress that fitted her magnificent figure like a skin.   But we are going ahead too fast: Jenny Brady will not be married for many days yet; she is still posing for Alida, who, as long as daylight lasts, is working as usual. The cartoon of the angels has long since been finished, and now all her energies are bent on the completion of her picture for the Society.   It is a quaint mediæval canvas glowing with rich æsthetic color, a dream of sad, pale languor, that had caught Alida's fancy in reading Swinburne's adaptation of "How Lisa Loved the King."

Jenny was the most sympathetic of models; she could look like a powerful avenging angel, or limp and clinging as a flower, as the case might be. The quaintness of her mediæval robes pleased her fancy, and she liked lying back among soft pillows, one hand stretched out as though just lightly passed over the strings of a tall Florentine lyre. She would talk sometimes, sometimes half dream, and often, weary with late hours, go fast asleep, her trained muscles keeping the pose. She had been asleep the most of one afternoon, and started awake with surprise when Alida said:

"Jenny, time's up."

She unwrapped the draperies in which she was bound and uncoiled her long hair from its "platters," as she

called the large plaits in which mediæval ladies did their hair on the
sides of their faces.   Refreshed by her
long sleep, she was gorgeously handsome; her white shoulders gleamed
from above her chemise and her glorious mane of auburn hair threw out
the milky whiteness of her skin.
Alida looked at her, thinking for the
thousandth time what a glowing bit
of color and form she was.

"You'll come and pose for me now
and then after you are married, won't
you, Jenny?" she said; "just to keep
my eye for color up to the mark."

Jenny laughed; she enjoyed being
admired.   Marriage in her station was
a good deal more of a game of give
and take than in higher circles.   She
didn't think Mr. Blair would mind
her doing anything she wanted to do,
and even if he did he surely wouldn't

object to her posing for Alida. Alida had given much thought to what she should give Jenny for a wedding gift. She thought the girl might like to have one of her sketches, but she wasn't sure; she sounded her, and found that it was the one thing more than all others that she craved. Jenny had no interrupting shopping to do this afternoon, so Alida gave her a big portfolio of water colors, telling her to pick out one she liked. She watched the girl bending over the portfolio, and made a hasty sketch on the side of the canvas of the back of her head and her superb Angelesque shoulders. Jenny looked through the portfolio and selected two or three to choose from.

"I can't decide a bit," she said at last, raising her head almost shyly. "To tell the truth, Miss Craig, there's

one I'd like to have better than any
of these, but I don't know as you'll
like to give it to me. It's that woman
on the wall. You see I've always
had to keep my eyes on her when I've
been posing; I thought she was awfully ugly at first, but somehow she
kind of growed on me. It had a look
of you, some way, and it would kind
of remind me of you and the posing."
She pointed to a photograph on the
wall as she spoke; it was a beautiful
Braun print of Mona Lisa.

Alida caught her breath; it was one
of the happiest moments of her life.
Had she really been such a good influence in the girl's life—had she really
unintentionally led her to think the
Mona Lisa beautiful?

"You can certainly have that; it's
a photograph, and I'll get you one like
it," she said warmly. "You can

have a water color too ; " and Jenny selected a little coast scene because Tom was fond of the sea.

The possession of the two pictures was a crowning glory of the Blairs' house, and they were hung in conspicuous positions in the little parlor, which was otherwise ornamented by a suit of red plush furniture and some gilt chairs and tables.

When Jenny had gone, Alida curled herself up, tired out, in a cushioned and pillowed corner by the fire. She lit a little lamp that was fastened into the woodwork at the head of her couch, and prepared for a happy hour with "The Newcomes." The soft light on her book grew indistinct as she read over the last chapters, which she almost knew by heart. She closed the book before she came to the chapter where the Colonel says " Adsum "

—her heart was too sore to read again those pathetic chapters. Her thoughts ran away to the old Grey Friars school, where she had gone one murky morning when in London. The little marble cloister, lined with tablets to its talented sons, the old building, the little chapel where Pendennis saw the old Colonel's bowed head at prayer, all came back to her. The children are gone from Grey Friars now, moved away into some more healthy locality; the place is very quiet save for the old pensioners. There was scarcely a sound in the building save the clatter of Alida's feet following the slow-paced old verger; he was a nice old man and had not hurried her, letting her sit for a moment in the old pew that Thackeray might have sat in when he was a boy. She had given him half a crown when she went away, and he had told her to come to afternoon service, that the singing was very fine. She never went—she liked best to think of the place peopled by the memories of those who, though they existed only on paper, were more real to her than the crowd that would come to listen to the Sunday music.

Ordinarily, cuddled up as she was in a nice warm corner, tired out with her day's work, Alida would have put her hands up under her chin, a baby-ish habit that she had never outgrown, and gone to sleep. But lately her fine nerves had become strangely out of her control, unless she was at work or with others. The glory of the pictures in the Louvre, of the Rembrandts and Velasquezs, was just the same, but somehow she could no longer dream of them by the hour, or be absolutely happy in the artistic working out of her pictures. She would take up a book as of old, but her thoughts would soon stray away from the printed page to other things, and then suddenly her whole soul would be crying Philip! Philip! Philip! She never imagined or thought that anything could possibly change, but as she had lived she expected always to go on, apart from the joys of ordinary life, the ties of home and of family love. In the revelation of her lover's first kiss she had realized the desolation of her lot. Night after night she sobbed herself to sleep, not in bitterness or complaining, but because something was lost, something which for twenty-four hours had brought her in touch with the world of men and women, making her half break from the spell which her rapt life had woven, making her personality quaint and interesting, but scarcely more of the nineteenth century than some faint lady on a faded tapestry. The intensity of her emotion prevented her keeping still any longer; she walked up and down, trying to stop thinking, thinking.

It was a relief at last when she heard the door of the next apartment close and a brisk step come down the hall. "I can't be alone like this," she thought. "It just kills me. There's Miss Wells going out to dinner, and it's such a rainy night. I wonder if she won't stay with me. Miss Wells—ah, Miss Wells!" she called, running and thrusting her head out of the door; "won't you come and dine with me? You'll certainly melt away if you go out in this pour. Chloe is concocting the most delicious gumbo; please come and share it."

"No reasonable offer refused," called back Miss Wells in a lively tone. "But just wait for a moment until I put away my umbrella and gums. You'll excuse evening dress, I presume, but if not I'll put on a white tie."

"You needn't mind about the tie."

"How jolly this is!" said Miss Wells, standing before the fire with her hands in her pockets, and gazing at the pretty table which Chloe had drawn up comfortably near the blazing logs. "I'd like to keep house myself if only I could find a twin sister of the invaluable Chloe. But the nine maids in one month, which was my last effort in the domestic line, have made me very well content with cheerless restaurant dinners. After all, a woman can't do everything. Sometimes I think it would be real nice to have a quiet, domestic little husband who would look after things while I was downtown. I'd make him feel real self-respecting—why, I'd give him an allowance. Gumbo!'' as Chloe set a soup plate down in front of her. ''Young woman, if you don't appreciate the blessing of a woman who can really make it, you deserve, late in life, to be catered for by a raw Swede—my ninth was a Swede.''

Miss Wells was about forty, of large and awful proportions; her dress fitted to a nicety, and though severely plain in design, was of the handsomest material, and showed the cut of a first-rate tailor. Her jacket opened over an immaculate shirt front and a doe-skin waistcoat.

''You should just see me once in a

tea gown," she had remarked to a friend who criticised the style of her dress. "I look like a baby elephant in a pillowcase."

Her round red face glowed with good health and spirits, and her smooth hair was cut in a severe bang across her forehead and rolled in a small club behind. She had held for years an important position in one of the large publishing houses, where her desk and all her affairs were always as thoroughly up to the mark as her appearance would suggest.

"Won't you carve?" said Alida, as, after some "fillet of sole" which Chloe had a habit of compounding out of plain American flounder, a nice little roast duck was brought on. "I carve so badly."

If Miss Wells had a weakness, it was her carving and her play at chess.

She laid the duck out now with the perfection of skill.

"A dinner of two and a duck is perfect," she said, "because every one gets the best piece. You artists are so delightful," she went on, as she filled up her beautiful Venetian glass again; "your things never match. Now I always used to have my things in sets until I came to live here; now I'm perfectly content with the débris the nine left me. Won't you ask yourself to have another piece of duck, as you are hostess?"

"No more, thank you," said Alida.

"You look pale—do you know it, my child? There are great rings under your eyes; you've been working too hard, I suppose. Is that the picture you're doing? Is it done? I always like an artist to tell me when things are done; one's never sure, especially lately; you wouldn't really think that things were commenced. I'm not really a judge, but I should suppose that it was very fine if one knew. I'm sure I hope that some one will buy it, and that you will get a real good price."

"It's not done yet, nothing like; there are lots of things to be done to it. Now, although you carve so well, I know you can't dress a salad. Wait until you see how this one turns out; I think you will like it;" mixing the oil and vinegar with great care, and tossing the contents of the great gold medallion bowl about thoroughly. "There, is that just right?"

"Perfection. A little more salt, please; there's nothing suits me quite like a Russian salad."

They finished dinner, and Alida made coffee in a little, shining brass coffee-pot that turned upside down in the most delightful way. She enjoyed Miss Wells's racy, good-humored accounts of her friends and their doings and sayings ; for Miss Wells knew everybody, and her plain face was welcomed in all sorts and conditions of houses.

"Have you been downstairs lately to see Mrs. Bohm?" she said, as she rose to go. "Katie, who chores for me, said this morning that her little boy was terribly sick. You know her, don't you?"

Alida's conscience smote her; wrapped up in her own sorrows, she had scarcely taken thought of those under the same roof.

"Know Mary Bohm—of course I do; we were students together in Paris. Oh, why haven't I been down to see her?" she cried, reproaching herself. "Do you think it is too late to go now?"

"Well, Katie said the child was terribly sick; it's awful her being there alone with him. I wanted to go myself, only I was afraid of intruding. You can see if there is a light in the room, and if there is, knock softly. If there is anything I can do, call on me. I sleep like a log, but I'm not afraid and I'll leave the door unlocked. Good-night, dear little girl." Then, as Alida sped downstairs to Mrs. Bohm's apartment, and Miss Wells unlocked her door, she said to herself: "Dear me, how slight and frail she is; she's fallen away in the last week; she ought to have someone to look after her. How I wish I was her mother. Wouldn't it be fine to have a great girl like that to come home to?"

CHAPTER X

Alida knocked softly twice on
Mrs. Bohm's door; she could see that
the gas was still lighted, but there
was no answer. Something impelled
her to turn the handle of the door,
which was unlocked, and she opened
it noiselessly and went in. As she
stood for a moment in the passage-
way that led into the studio, she
could hear the little boy crying pite-
ously.

"Mary—Mary Bohm," she said
softly; "it is I, Alida Craig."

Mrs. Bohm came out of the studio;
her black dress emphasized the pallor
of her face and the great rings under

her eyes; she was very handsome,
though, in spite of her disordered garments, and the fact that her wonderful yellow hair was half falling down
her back.

"I'm all in disorder," she said, putting her hand up to her head. "But
Tommy's been so ill that I've been up
night and day; I'm half sick for
sleep." She spoke in pretty, soft
tones that were yet oddly marked by
a decided Western accent.

"I'll stay and sit by Tommy while
you get some rest," said Alida, and
walked down the hall to the studio.
She started back on the threshold
almost involuntarily, and then went
in.

Mrs. Bohm followed her. "Yes,"
she said, looking around at the room,
that was absolutely bare of furniture
save for a big easel on which stood a

large canvas, and a paint box, " I've had a hard time this winter. I've sold all my pretty things. I don't mind your knowing it now. I suppose I haven't any pride left, though I've kept quiet and not answered your knock lots of times this winter, for fear you'd know."

The child broke out again in a wailing cry, and Alida went into the bedroom where he lay. He was without fever now, but wasted and worn, and kept moaning.

" Make him another poultice, Alida," said Mary, sinking down into a chair beside the bed. " It's pneumonia, and there's nothing to do but keep up the poultices. I'm so worn out that I forgot it, and the last one must be cold."

Alida was thankful that she had had her experience with nursing Chloe to rely upon. She lighted the little gas lamp and soon had the nice hot poultice, not too hard or too soft, according to the best directions, all ready. The child breathed easier when she had put it on his chest, and closed his eyes in comfort and satisfaction.

"Mary, keep your eyes open just a moment," she said ; "I must go upstairs for something."

She fled up to her own apartment, and unlocking the sideboard found a bottle of good old port; then she cut some nice thin slices of bread and some cold duck, and in less time than it takes to tell was back in the bedroom again carrying a nicely arranged little tray.

"Have some port, Mary, and eat some of those sandwiches ; there's no use trying to take care of Tommy by making yourself ill too."

Tommy was fast asleep now, breath-
ing hard and heavily, and the poor
tired woman gladly drank the wine.
The color began to creep back into
her cheeks, and the sickening faint
feeling left her.

"I was faint, I guess," she said.
"Alida Craig, you've come like an
angel."

"Go out in the studio and lie down;
we can put this cot out there, and
then if Tommy wakes he won't disturb
you. Come, I'll fix it."

The weary woman lay down on the
little pallet, and Alida sat beside her,
looking into the room beyond, where
the child was asleep. For a little
while all was quiet, then Mrs. Bohm
began to talk. The wine had rested
her body and the terrible sleeplessness
had left her. She needed to talk, to
tell some one of her sufferings—about

the winter. When her husband died she had come home from Paris, and settled in New York. She had taken this apartment in the Sherburne studio building because she knew it was one of the best buildings, had sent her pictures around to the exhibitions, had sent word about that she would give lessons, etc., and had waited. If the exhibitions hung her work, which they did not always do, her pictures never sold, and day by day she had used up her small capital until now it was almost gone. Her family had written her again and again to come out to them, but she still lingered, hoping that something would yet turn up.

"Where do your family live?" said Alida, a thrill at the thought of going home passing over her.

"Washburn, Indiana," bitterly;

"and they don't know a painting from a chromo. I'd rather die than go back there. You're the strangest girl, Alida; you've always been so lucky; the way you used to have number one in the concours month after month, and the luck you've had since you came home; yet I've always felt that you never cared half so much about your work as I did. Why, I've half starved to stay here these last two months and paint a picture for the Society. It's almost done—there on the easel."

Alida did not speak; she went into the next room and made another poultice for Tommy. Poor, pretty Mary Bohm! she remembered her at Julian's working night and day, absolutely devoured with ambition, yet always failing miserably.

"Is Tommy all right?"

" Yes, dear."

" I'll go to sleep in a moment; I'm beginning to be quite drowsy. I want you to do something for me."

" Yes."

" Light a candle—there's one on the mantelpiece—and look at the picture. I'd sleep easier if I really had some one's opinion." She sat up with wide-open eyes while Alida steadied the flickering light to see the canvas. It was a madonna and child, more poorly than badly painted; the color was tinged with a soft, unpleasant butteriness, and there was not one line of interest or originality about it.

"I think it's the best thing you have done, but I don't want to say any more until I have seen it by daylight," was all Alida could say to the anxious, inquiring face awaiting her decision.

That was enough, however; it was treating the picture seriously, and Mary soon fell asleep, satisfied that the child was doing well, and that this last picture would bring the success she craved.

"Poor Mary," thought Alida. "Why did she ever go away from the farm in Indiana? Why did she have the art fever? I'm going to see if Bertha won't persuade Philip to establish a scholarship to send girls home to America who will give up studying art. It's the only thing for most of them to do." It was hard work for Alida to keep awake; she was not used to watching, and the room was so still that she nearly dropped off without thinking; then she roused herself with a start and made the poultice again. She began to be afraid that she would not be able to hold out much longer, and she thought she would wake Mary soon, and run up and call Chloe. She thought it must be nearly morning, but just then the clock struck one.

Rosamond Wells, for such was the title that her godparents had bestowed upon that plain and cheery damsel, was awakened in the middle of the night by some one shaking her violently.

"My watch is—" she began. "Oh, it's you, Alida Craig. Is the child worse—what can I do?"

"His mother's afraid he's dying; he's suddenly taken worse. Would you go out with Chloe for the doctor? Chloe, you know, can't find her way around New York one bit."

"Where is it?"

"Fifty-eighth Street."

"Don't you mind about Chloe, I'm

not one bit afraid to go by myself; only wake her up and have her go down to Mrs. Bohm's. There's some whiskey in that closet ; you'd better give me a drop and take some yourself; you're a ghost."

As she spoke, Miss Wells was dragging on her clothes, and it speaks well for her style of garments that they were as easily gotten into as a man's; and at half-past two in the morning, with only five minutes at her disposal, she looked as neat and trim as ever.

" You ought not to go alone," said Alida, distressed. "Suppose some one should stop you ? "

" Nonsense, child; at the rate I'll go they'll think I am an escaped lunatic. If they did stop me, I'd just say, ' I'm going for the doctor; wait here until I come back and I'll blow your head off.' Good-by, I'll be back in ten minutes." And fastening on her billycock hat as she went along, Miss Wells sped away faster than from her girth one would have deemed possible.

The sick-room was now a serious battle-ground, where the conflict of life and death was being fought out. The doctor came, bringing his healthy, comforting presence to sustain their fainting hopes. He turned every one out of the room excepting Chloe, and the three women sat in the bare studio, looking at the weak "Madonna and Child," hour after hour, until the cold gray dawn crept in at the great north window.

"I'll make some coffee," said Alida at last, rising. But she was so stiff and tired that she could scarcely move.

Miss Wells sprang to her feet.

" I'll make it ; and, Mrs. Bohm, do light a fire, it's perishingly cold."

In a few minutes the doctor came out of the sick-room.

" The child is doing well now," he said gravely. " Unless something unforeseen arises he will get along now. Thank you, Miss Wells," as he took the cup of coffee from her hand and seated himself beside the blazing fire. " This is indeed comfortable after being up so long."

" You are sure that Tommy will get well ? " said Mrs. Bohm.

" Yes, quite sure ; only when he is recovered I should advise a country life. He's rather a delicate child. I wouldn't try to bring him up in the city. Now, ladies, good-morning; go to bed and sleep as long as you can, as I am going to do. I'll be around in the afternoon; your maid will stay with the child until I can send a nurse, I believe. Good-morning."

Now that the strain was over, Mrs. Bohm let Alida take her upstairs, and they breakfasted in strange pot-luck fashion and went to bed, excepting Miss Wells, who was due down-town, and who, having taken a cold plunge and put on a fresh shirt front and collar, appeared at her work at the usual hour as immaculate and trim as ever.

"Up since three in the morning and I've never turned a hair," was her comment as she locked her desk when evening came, not one second earlier than usual.

But among all these studio people we must not forget the other train of our story, and that we have another invalid who has been getting better while we have been talking about others. In truth, Madame Fremiet's illness was of short duration, and in a few days she appeared again at the theatre, to all appearances as well as ever. Those, however, who knew her intimately realized that a great change had come over her. Mixed into her Creole blood there was an odd strain of super-nervousness, call it what you will, that resulted in a sixth sense amounting almost to second sight. It was not the ordinary presentiment of a nervous woman— no, only two or three times in her life had the veil of everyday events been wiped away, and she had seemed to see into the future; once just before she had taken the momentous step of leaving her home to go upon the stage. Now she saw nothing clearly; she only felt a negation of all her future wishes and desires. Even when she had recovered her health to

all outward seeming, her mind was in
a dream, groping about for some
vague clew—the mystery of she knew
not what—which she realized she
might stumble across at any moment.
Her lips were closed on the subject of
her inward emotions; she could not
speak of them even to Philip; her
manner toward him was the same as
before, though she absolutely refused
to speak with any decision of their
wedding day.

Philip, seeing how agitated she became at the pressing of his suit, spoke
of it no more. In the languor that
had crept over her in her days of con-
valescence, she seemed more charming
to him than ever. He little realized
that she received each token of his
love and devotion with a pang of sadness ; that firmly rooted in her mind
was the feeling that their attachment

was almost over ; that their seven
years of waiting was in vain, and that
they would never be man and wife.
The better Margaret's physical condition became, the more firmly rooted
grew all these ideas. Her engagement
at the theatre was drawing to a close,
and she still seemed no nearer the
realization of her vision than before.

The Duke of Axminster had not
returned to England, as he had intended to do on hearing of Margaret's
engagement to Philip Herford. As
soon as she was well enough, Margaret sent him a little note, and the
following morning he came up to the
Plaza. Their interview was very trying, and required all Margaret's tact ;
yet somehow—and it was a difficult
thing to do, for Axminster was not
famous for flights of the imagination

—she made him understand just how she felt.

"Don't feel," she said, "that I am throwing Mr. Herford over for you, or that I shall marry you because I do not marry Mr. Herford. I just know that this thing will be; that it is my fate, and that we must all accept it. But time must work out the problem as it will; I cannot hurry it; I don't know anything."

The Duke walked up and down the room slowly ; it was the intensest nervousness that his phlegmatic temperament could show.

"It's all very wonderful," he said. "I don't understand it, and I do. It's an awkward position for me, but since you say Herford would gladly be released, I do not see that I am harming him in any attitude that I take. I am good at waiting, and I might just as well go up to the Adirondacks to shoot for a little while as go home to England. Besides, it will be easier to get back from there; all you will have to do is to wire, 'Come.'"

The simplicity of his almost boy-ish affection touched Margaret, as it had done many times before.

"Oh, Duke," she said, "why cannot I love you in return? Why am I giving myself to you so coldly? I despise myself ; it is sacrificing you. I ought not to marry you."

There was a certain tightening about his mouth, that those who had seen him in the thick of battle, when he was a cadet of his house and Lieu-tenant of the 9th ——, might remember.

"You don't know at all," he said. "I accepted it so long ago that it's more than I ever hoped or dreamed for that you would be my wife at all. I'm happy, happy—do you understand? I don't care whether you love me or not; I don't want to think of it or talk of it; I love you, that's enough, that's all."

She was not yet very strong, and the talking had wearied her; her beautiful face was pale. He longed to take her up in his arms and carry her away, his possession, captured by right of strength and devotion. Instead, he bent down, kissing her hand.

"Good-by, my duchess," he said.

CHAPTER XI

These were busy days for Alida. Tommy progressed but slowly, and all the time that she could spare was devoted to amusing him and helping to cheer up his mother. Mrs. Bohm had relapsed into her old, hard, sullen manner ; she relieved the nurse and wrote a good many letters, but she had not touched paints and brushes since the night of the child's crisis. The dreary "Madonna and Child" still stared blankly from the easel, unfinished and unvarnished, although the time was nearing when pictures for the Society were to be judged. Miss Wells had been, as from the first, a well-balanced guardian angel. She brought the newest toys for Tommy, took no notice of Mrs. Bohm's mood, and finally, like an electric shock, started the subject of the "Madonna," about which the poor woman was eating out her heart.

"I suppose it's finished now," she said one evening; for, truth to tell, she knew no more of painting than a bat, and had never noticed the picture particularly.

Mrs. Bohm looked up from her sewing and then she began to cry, to Miss Wells's great distress.

"It's never going to be finished; I haven't worked on it for a long time," she said at last. "Perhaps you don't know how bad it is, but it's awful. I saw it just as plain as day the night Tommy was so sick.

All my things have been bad straight from the start. I used to hate Alida when she was in Julian's, the way she got ahead. I wanted to succeed so, to get ahead of every one, to be admired. That isn't Art, and I don't wonder I didn't do any better. I've never had the least notion of the real thing, like that little creature upstairs, who lives in her work."

"She's a good girl and gentle and modest," said Miss Wells, for lack of anything else to say ; and she listened patiently to the poor woman's story, of the petty jealousies and triumphs and excitements that she had thought made up an artist's life, never seeing that she was thinking of nothing but herself. Now, thank heaven, she was wiser, and all her plans were ready to take Tommy home to the old farm in Indiana. The tears came into her eyes, and perhaps into Miss Wells's too, as she finished her confession.

"I've thought my painting very fine," she said, "but I don't believe it's any too good for Indiana. They're proud of me out there, and I guess, after all, home's the best place for most women."

So, as soon as Tommy was able to be moved, he was taken down to the Grand Central Station in a carriage, with Alida and Miss Wells on the front seat, and toys and picture-books enough to last a journey around the world.

"It will seem lonely without them," said Miss Wells, as the train moved out of the station. "Though I declare, for all the tramping up and down stairs and bearing with that poor girl's temper, you look stronger than you did. You needn't worry about her; she's taken off her black, I notice, and when a girl starts off on a journey with as well-fitting a gown as that, it shows that she is beginning to pick up. Now, you'd better come and lunch with me. If I've money enough left after buying that leaping kangaroo we'll go to Del's. And I've two seats for the Lohengrin matinee. I'd like you to come with me ever so much—that is, if you're not so musical that you want a score. I hate a score."

" No," said Alida ; " I don't know one note from another, but I should love to hear Lohengrin again."

" Come along, then; there's nothing like the opera for me. I go and blubber, and I love it all straight up from the swan. As for the dragon in Siegfried, I'm devotedly attached to it.   Let's walk down, the sunshine is so inviting, and I have my best necktie on, which always makes me feel a cut above the Fourth Avenue car."

The sunshine was truly so enticing that many other people were tempted out.   Among them Margaret went out, on a round of shopping.   Coming home, as she passed the tall building where Alida had her studio, it reminded her of her former visit to the little artist girl.   Her illness coming so soon after had driven all thought of the portrait, and the absurdity of the anonymous letter, quite out of her mind.   She had promised Miss Craig to sit for the portrait when she stopped playing; now there was only a week longer of her engagement at the Fifth Avenue, and it seemed a very good opportunity to arrange for the sittings.   No sooner

thought than done: she stopped the
carriage and went up the long flights
of stone stairs that led to Alida's
apartment. Margaret wore, as she
often did when she went about alone,
a thick, dark veil, and all the way
going upstairs she was struggling to
unfasten its tangled ends. Miss Craig
was not at home, the old colored
woman said who opened the door for
her; perhaps she would leave a message. Margaret was tired from mount-
ing the stairs, so she said she would
come in for a moment and write a
note. Chloe went to Alida's desk,
found a sheet of paper and a pencil,
and while she was getting them Margaret at last succeeded in unpinning
the reluctant veil; she took off her
right glove too, and sat down in a
chair which happened to be placed
directly under the broad, sweeping

glare of the skylight. It took Chloe some time to find the paper, and as she turned around, murmuring many apologies for her mistress's absence, her face became suddenly ashen gray ; the paper and pencil fell from her trembling old hands.

"Lor' sakes," she murmured, with chattering teeth. "Lor' sakes, it's Mam'zell Margaret."

Margaret arose from her chair. Twenty years had gone by, changing Chloe from a buxom, strong woman to an old one with bent figure and white wool, but Madame Fremiet would have known the voice anywhere — the voice of the negress who had been her nurse, who had dressed her on her wedding day, and who had gone with her to the new home ; the one link that bound her to her happy childhood in the stormy

years of her life with Monsieur Bonaventure.

"Chloe, Chloe, my dear, dear
Chloe!" she cried, enthusiastically
clasping the old woman.

For a few moments they clung to
each other, murmuring an unintelli-
gible babble of patois, words long forgotten. Baby phrases that Chloe had
taught her rushed upon Margaret's
lips; the old negress sobbed with joy.
Madame Fremiet at last released
Chloe's clinging hands and sat down
again in the chair.

"How beautiful you is!" murmured the old woman, feasting her
eyes on her nursling. "You isn't a
day older than you was, 'pears to me.
There weren't never no one as pretty
as you. Old Chloe never thought her
old eyes would see you again."

The genuine love that shone in her

faded orbs brought tears to Margaret's bright ones. She asked the old woman about her life, and what she had been doing all these years, wondering how she happened to be in service with Miss Craig.

"Won't you come back again and be my maid?" she said; "you know you really belong to me." She was surprised that Chloe looked grave, almost pained, for a moment.

"I can't leave Miss 'Lida," she said. "I b'longed to you sure 'nuff, Mam'zell, but I can't leave Miss' Lida; she belongs to me, I've had her ever since she was born."

"Ever since she was born!" repeated Margaret. The words died on her lips, and to hide her confusion she broke out in a torrent of questions.

When had Chloe left New Orleans?

What had she done all the time? When had she met Miss Craig? She asked everything excepting the question that was nearest her heart. So this was Chloe, old and wrinkled, the Chloe she had seen last sitting in the big, low nursery at Los Portos. How many nights since then the picture had come back to her, and she had wakened from troubled dreams of the little toddling white baby on Chloe's knee, who had crowed and laughed and clutched at the diamonds on her neck when she had gone in to say goodnight, decked out in all her jewels and finery to receive her guests on what proved to be her last night under her husband's roof. "Chloe, do you remember my last night at home?" she said.

"Yes," said Chloe gravely. There was a ring of reproach in the old woman's words that stung Margaret; she arose, pacing the room in excitement; she tried to explain and excuse her departure, but before the simple black servant her motives appeared inadequate.

"Chloe," she said, "you know how miserable my marriage was; I was so excited and happy with my success in the play that night, that I fairly forgot how terrible Monsieur Bonaventure could be, and I went to him, radiant with success, thinking he would sympathize with me and let me go on the stage. He was terrible, and we had a most fearful quarrel; we had had so many quarrels and had said so many bitter things that I suppose he thought he could say anything he liked, but he went a little too far that night, and I was so angry that I walked straight out of the house."

Chloe knelt down beside Margaret and patted one of her hands as she would have done a baby's. She was a very ignorant old woman, who had been taught a certain sense of right and wrong. She had been abroad and travelled with Alida, but her New Orleans patois had never changed into good Parisian French, and she still spoke very Southern English. For twenty years she had nursed a perfectly just resentment against Margaret for deserting her child, but now that she saw again her beloved mistress, her old love got the better of her convictions. That's what these good black creatures are made for ; they are all heart and warm affection. She didn't exactly comprehend why Margaret should choose to desert her baby, but then, since she had chosen, why shouldn't she?

"There, there," said the old woman, patting her hand, "did you ever think your baby would be a woman grown now if she had lived?"

"If she had lived! Chloe, did she live? Do you know anything of her? I've never heard a word of my old home since that night. At first my thoughts were full of my studies and my successes, but lately I've not been well, and it's all come back to me—fancies that I would like to see the old place again, to see you and to hear of my daughter. Perhaps I could tell her, and she could understand, that I was unhappy and repressed at home, that I was born for the stage and could no more help going than the birds from flying. Perhaps she would forgive me, and even be proud of me."

"Did you never hear from Massa

all this time?" said Chloe in amazement. "Certainly he was a hard man."

"Hard and unforgiving. But he is dead; he sent me a message from his death-bed, thanking me for never having played in New Orleans."

"So he's dead," said Chloe. She had always hated her old master, and her judgment upon him was proportionately severe. "So he's dead. He was a hard man ; he turned me out of doors with the baby, Mam'zell, the day after you went away ; he was like the devil himself. I thought he'd kill me and the child, and they said he burnt up every scrap of your dresses and things that you left. He gave me a little bit of money every year to take care of the child, but he swore me never to tell her who she

was ; he even made me give her another name.''

Margaret's eyes met the old woman's ; she looked at her firmly for a
moment, then she put out her hand,
steadying herself against the arm of a
chair.

''My baby's name was Margaret,
like mine.''

''I called her Alida,'' said Chloe
huskily.

Her words reached Margaret
faintly.

''Alida ! Alida !'' she cried. The
terrible pain at her heart was grip-
ping her with exhausting agony ; a
feeling of suffocation arose in her
throat, and she fainted in Chloe's
arms. Chloe was too good a nurse to
be frightened ; she chafed the poor
cold hands and poured brandy between the clenched teeth, working

over her with untiring zeal. At last the color crept back into Margaret's face; she opened her eyes. "Tell me all about her," she said.

And Chloe told her all about Alida : tales of her childhood that went to the poor mother's heart—poor Margaret, who had never seemed to have a mother's heart until now. She listened enraptured as Chloe told how, from a baby, Alida was always drawing pictures, and how when she was only twelve years old she had painted some Christmas cards for a little book-shop, and how, when Chloe and Alida had gone to get the money for them, the kindly shopkeeper, amazed at the diminutive artist, had told her that she should study in an art school. Then the little maiden had studied up the question of art schools until kindly fate had led her footsteps to the Art Students' League. Chloe told, too, of their going abroad, and of her having pneumonia and how Alida nursed her; besides many other things which were like a strange story to Margaret's ears.

As I have said, Chloe was ignorant, so ignorant as to be absolutely honest. When Monsieur Bonaventure had made her swear never to tell Alida her real name, Chloe had never thought of disobeying his injunctions. She thought of him as so nearly one remove from a demon that she believed if she broke her word he would surely fulfil his threat of no longer sending the thousand dollars a year for his daughter's support. Perhaps the bitterest drop in Margaret's cup was that, while she had had hundreds of thousands of dollars, jewels, rich dresses, every luxury, her child had grown up half fed, half clothed, on a miserable pittance, eked out by what her nimble fingers and clever brain could supply—grown up as the lilies grow—to be a lily in the midst of common weeds ; to catch her education somehow, and to be indebted, save for the breath she drew, to no one but her own good impulses, and one old, loving servant.

But Chloe, having told all the details of her nursling's life, was not yet done; in the old woman's slow brain there had stuck fast one fact : the coming and strange departure of Alida's one lover ; and she poured out all her hopes and fears for Alida's marrying Mr. Herford. Margaret listened as in a dream as Chloe recounted his daily visits, and his goodness, and how he had suddenly ceased coming, and that she could see under all Alida's singing and working that something was wrong.

"I am judged," thought Margaret. She felt that her presentiment had come to be fulfilled; she did not know what she should do; the complication was too terrible to be thought out quickly.

"Chloe," she said, rising, "you have kept your promise to Monsieur Bonaventure very faithfully. I want you to keep a promise to me. You must never, never let Alida know that I am her mother."

But Chloe could not understand. It was the dream of her life to see her two charges together; she begged Margaret to let her tell Alida at once; but Margaret was so earnest that the faithful old woman promised at last.

"And you so sick, too, Mam'zell,"

was her only reproach. "She'd be such a comfort to you." But Margaret only kissed her and turned away, her face growing very white, and there was a queer dim smile hanging around her lips as she went downstairs from Alida's studio. Her dress, sweeping the floor, seemed to be whispering good-by to the little daughter she had seen but once.

For days Margaret could come to no solution of her difficult position. On one point alone she was decided. She had abandoned her baby, and left her unloved and uncared for during all the years of her young, tender life; for that there was no reparation, and, she felt, no forgiveness. But in the future Alida must be happy; the child must marry Philip. Yet even in the thought lay subtle difficulties that baffled her penetration. Margaret longed for her daughter; she did not feel herself capable of carrying out her first intention, which she had told Chloe, of never disclosing her identity to Alida ; for Margaret was a strict Catholic, and the church requires of its daughters an accounting of their children and their children's children. She spent many hours at her *prie Dieu* looking for light and strength, and yet her duty was such a divided one that she could come to no decision. It would be a shock to any girl to discover that her husband had formerly been affianced to her mother, and to a girl as delicate and poetic as Alida the idea would be ghastly and horrible. These circumstances turned themselves over and over in the poor mother's brain, and she might have put herself at last in the hands of her amiable father confessor—in which case this story might have had a somewhat entangled ending—had she not received an opportune visit from her lawyer, Mr. Barlow.

Mr. Barlow's errand was one from which he shrank, and which he felt required the utmost delicacy. In settling Monsieur Bonaventure's estate, which had been left to the Jesuit Monastery just outside of New Orleans, he had come across the records of a daughter born to Margaret and Charles Antoine Gabrille Bonaventure, but beyond that there was no mention of the child's death, nor any trace in Monsieur Bonaventure's effects of her existence. Mr. Barlow's legal mind refused to accept as dead any one whose burial certificate was not registered; and at the risk of stirring up sad, long-buried memories in Madame Fremiet's heart, he had felt obliged to come and ask her to clear up the mystery, which, if from no other point of view, affected the titles and estates of Monsieur Bonaventure's princely gift to the monastery. The kindness of Mr. Barlow's tone, the absolute fineness of his feeling for her, and the gravity of his face, as he told her very simply the object of his visit, soothed Margaret's aching heart into a clear knowledge that she must act now, once and forever.

"The fathers, what do they say?" she said inquiringly.

"That the child is dead. Monsieur Bonaventure told them so on his death-bed; her existence would invalidate their bequest."

Margaret rose, walked wearily up and down the room once or twice, then seated herself again opposite Mr.

Barlow, with the clear light from a window falling full on her face.

"Mr. Barlow," she said, "there is no record of the child's death—that I know—and yet she is dead. If the fathers are content with their possession, very well ; strengthen them in the belief that the child died shortly after I left New Orleans. I am willing, if necessary, to add to the legacy if it will aid in keeping the very sad events of my early life undisturbed in their oblivion."

Her tone was so grave and full of sorrow that once more Mr. Barlow was touched by her simple womanly dignity. He rose to go, feeling that before the wounded heart of a bereaved mother there was little place for the law of codes and courts.

CHAPTER XII

Margaret's mind was made up: the church had its due in the rich estate of Monsieur Bonaventure ; her one duty now was to make Alida happy. She spent the night thinking and planning, for she had decided that not only must Philip leave her, but he must leave her without a pang. She was too great, if the sacrifice must be made, not to make it utter and complete. She would have no sentimental parting with her lover. She lay awake that night trying to think what was the surest way of making the break between them final. Evidently the night brought a solution of her difficulties, for she slept toward morning, and when she arose the weight of care was gone; she looked better than for many weeks, and Barnes noticed that she displayed a wonderful interest in her toilet.

When Philip came to pay his daily visit, he was delighted at her evident improvement in health and spirits. He had been much troubled by her depression and unhappiness, and by a feeling that she was shutting herself away from him; now she was again her old self. She wore a long, flowing gown, of burnished-copper color, that showed glimpses of her white arms and neck, and a bit of copper-colored ribbon in her dark locks added a touch of coquetry to her appearance. Margaret had thought out her plan deeply and well. She was a woman, therefore more or less able to conceal or control her feelings; and beyond that, she was a great actress, and in entering the room she had taken up a rôle which she intended to play through. Now that the struggle of her decision was over, she felt perfectly calm; quite as she would have felt at playing a new part. As Philip watched the charm of her languorous beauty, and thought her every movement exquisitely graceful and unstudied, Margaret was bringing every inch of her artistic training to keep within the lines that she had laid down for herself.

Mr. Howells has cleverly stated the axiom that no man can be in love with more than two women at once. I don't know whether or not he goes on to state that those women must appeal to very different sides of the man's nature, and that, as in this instance, there is never the slightest doubt of which is the overwhelming passion. Philip would have been something more than human if he had not felt the delicious charm, half coquetry, half regalness, which blended in Margaret's manner. She was more at ease with him than for many a long day, and chatted away with the *abandon* of a happy child. The scintillating brilliancy of her dark eyes shone with a soft, alluring light, and when she laughed it was with the gay, happy ring of one who is content and at peace. She was herself, her best, richest, most captivating self, exerting carelessly and idly the strong magnetic influence that had made whole theatres of people acknowledge her magic, before which princes and people bowed alike. She was as beautiful as in the first days when Philip had come on his wooing.

"You seem in a melting mood to-day, Margaret," he said at last. "You've only three more nights to play, and yet we seem as far from our wedding day as ever. I would not have thought you would be so coquettish; tell me when you will be mine?"

Margaret leaned back, and looking at him with dreamy, half-closed eyes, she smiled a delicious, mischievous smile.

"Never!" she said.

Philip thought it was some jest, and yet there was a ring in her voice that was very far from joking.

"Margaret, what do you mean?" he said.

"I mean what I say, Philip. We have been such ideal lovers, why marry and have all the romance taken away?   I really don't mean to marry you ; I'm in earnest.   In fact "—she arose and stood looking at him with grave dignity—"I don't think you have cared for me much lately.   You know things travel so easily ; I've heard all about Miss Craig and your devotion to her.   Ah, Philip," she said mockingly, "you always had such good taste in the fine arts ; having wearied of the footlights, have you found fresh charms in the palette and brushes?"

Philip's position was a terrible one. A weaker man would have defended the position, have explained, and——. Philip said nothing for a few seconds, then he spoke very quietly.

"Margaret, this is unworthy of you.   It's not like you to be jealous; you are my affianced wife; you have had all my love and devotion for years; why should you be jealous?''

''One often doesn't possess qualities until occasion develops them.'' Flippantly: ''I have never had any cause to be jealous until now.''

''Trust me now, dear.''

Philip went toward her, intending to solve the difficulty of the position by an embrace, but she moved a little away; then she seemed to have a quick repentance, and leaned against his shoulder, slipping her soft hand into his.

''Philip, do you really love me? Tell me so once more, won't you?'' she murmured.

Philip raised her hand and kissed it.

''I love you, Margaret,'' he said.

For a moment they were silent and stood together, Margaret quite carried outside of her part by the warm pressure of his kiss; then she snatched her hand away, and looking up into his face mischievously, said :

"Well, I don't love you ; I'm tired of you. I didn't know how tired until it came to my taking the irrevocable step of marrying you." It sounded simply vulgar as she said it, and she threw into her face an expression of vulgarity. For the first time it struck Philip that her large features were handsome to coarseness, and that her figure was voluptuous and sensuous. Margaret went on, speaking hurried- ly : "It is better to hurt your vanity and mine than to go on and find that we have made a terrible mistake ; you know that we all have two sides to our natures. I don't think that you have ever quite realized the other side of mine. You have appealed to what is best in me, fostered it, brought it out ; but the other side is there, and lately it has come uppermost. I love power and fame and glory; and just as years ago I walked out of my home without a pang, and left it to go on the stage, so, now that my stage life must come to an end, I cannot settle down to the dull round that you call society in New York ; I must have more power and position than you can give me. I can leave you as easily as I took that other step, to have what I most desire in my new life. Love you ! "—there was a ring of scorn in her voice—" I love you !— I love myself. I think it is better to have a real coronet of strawberry leaves than a crown of withered sentiments. Will you be the first to congratulate the future Duchess of Axminster ? "

Philip's quietness surprised even himself. He had noticed lately a hardness in Margaret that was new to his knowledge of her. Had it all then been merely a preparation for this extraordinary revelation of her character? She had always been moody and variable, changing as a chameleon from one point of view to another. Had it not been for the intensity of her passionate utterance, he could scarcely have thought her in earnest.

"Margaret, my dear," he said quietly, "I do not think you quite mean that being my wife wouldn't somewhat palliate the dulness of New York society. I don't know exactly what you mean, except that you have taken some jealous freak about Miss Craig. As you say, my dear, we all have two sides to our natures, and I can scarcely think that one so generous-hearted as yourself would think it the worst side of mine that I befriended a little, helpless, hard-working girl, whose chief attraction, when I first met her, was that she reminded me vaguely of you."

"We may talk all day, Philip," said Margaret, folding her large arms over her bosom to hide the wild beating of her heart, "but it cannot change the fact that I am tired of you, and that, to tell the truth, you are tired of me. As long as I thought you adored me, I fancied myself indispensable ; you see even in me there remains a vestige of the eternally feminine unnecessary sacrifice. When I heard of your devotion to Miss Craig I saw clearly that I had worn out my charmingly æsthetic but hardly human passion for you. Do you think that my heart, which has beat to the admiration of thousands, would be content with the perfunctory attentions of a husband who had wearied of me as a lover?" She sat down wearily in a chair. "Go and marry your little artist and live in Arcadia, and I will go and be a duchess"— with a graceful wave of her hand, as though the subject was dismissed.

That was the one point in the question that Philip could not understand; she certainly would not go to the length of saying that she was going to marry Axminster unless she was in earnest.

"Margaret, you have never been heartless ; if you have decided that you do not love me, and that you do love Axminster, say so ; let us part, if we must, in kindness and respect."

It was the crowning touch of her

sacrifice. Her nerves were like fine
steel, tense and strong. She stood
silent, fluctuating emotions chasing
over her face, that would have told
Philip even better than words that her
heart was no longer his. He felt
what she wanted to tell him, even
before, with a little gesture of shame
for her weakness, she came toward
him and laid her hand on his arm,
looking into his eyes with her beautiful ones, that seemed full of humilia-
tion at her confession.

"I do love Axminster, Philip ; I
was glad when I heard that you had
grown attached to Miss Craig. We
have lived in a dream of a vague poetic
fancy, but that is not the way I love
Axminster." And a tender and
beautiful smile fluttered around her
lips as she spoke.

So it was dead—their passion ;

dead ; never to be revived. The bare branches leaf out again in the spring ; but a worn-out passion—nothing can revive it.

"I hope you will be happy, dear," he said, and for the last time he bent and kissed her hand. "Good-by."

Margaret remained motionless, standing where he had left her, kissing the cold hand that his lips had pressed. "I shall never act so well again," she thought.

CHAPTER XIII

To all readers who object to the chapters regarding Alida, beginning with the fact that she was at work, I would like to say that they show great ignorance concerning the ways of artist folk, for what should a self-respecting artist be doing save painting as long as the daylight lasts? It is true that an artist's time is his own, and that when the mood strikes him he will lie fallow for long days ; but especially in the winter, with exhibitions coming on and orders dropping in, their hours are pretty regular, and " No admittance before four o'clock " on a door means that they have no minds for sociability or any kind of interruption. After all, is not an artist's life a pleasant one? is it not a true life to be able to indulge one's fancies and paint one's pictures all day long? Even the illustrating and stained-glass windows bring lots of fun. There is a pride and power of doing and seeing the thing grow. Blessed be these means of bread-winning, and the papers and cheap magazines which give young authors and artists a chance to cut their teeth and live.

I once heard a weak, artistically inclined lady promulgate a theory that all artists should be supported by the state. Save the mark! What did she know of the enthusiasms inspired by an earning money to pay a gas bill, of cartoons finished to pay the rent, of verses written to stay the clamors of the coal man, of the flush of joy

over a big, big check? If our enthusiasms, our ideals, are so slight that the
breath of the world dissipates them,
let them go; it is only an amateur's
mood that must be coddled carefully ;
the true artist is the journeyman
carving the gargoyles and pinnacles
of the cathedral into beauty ; nothing
is too small for his hand. Lay comfort to yourselves, ye who make your
daily bread out of your studies of the
beautiful ; did not Thackeray write
his lines, "At the Church Porch,"
for a lady's annual?

Alida, then, had been working all
day, and was tired, as she was every
day ; she had scraped up her palette
and put her things away, but her eyes
and thoughts were still full of her picture. "How Lisa Loved the King"
was finished ; the name and the date
were signed in the corner; on the

morrow the carters would take it away to be judged by the jury of the Society of American Artists. Then would come the supreme, the palpitating week before she knew if it was accepted, or if it was in the doubtful list, and might possibly be hung, if there was room. Several of the men who had studios in the building were on the jury, and she knew they would come and tell her the picture's fate as soon as it was decided. When her door-bell rang she thought it was Dorothy, and called out gayly from the chair where she sat behind the big canvas :

"Come, Dorothy, and see the picture ; it's signed and finished."

There was a man's quick step on the floor ; Chloe had gone away quietly; Alida rose, her face flushed with surprise to see Philip. She thought something terrible must have happened to Mrs. Beckington or Dorothy.

"What is the matter? Why did you come?"

Come! The sight of the familiar studio, the pictures, Alida's smooth palette with the dirty brushes sticking through it, brought a lump into Philip's throat; he scarcely dared look at her; everything was swept away; it seemed as though he had never been separated from her. Why explain, why talk! *She* was there.

"I—I came for some tea. What a glorious picture; are you going to send it to the Society?" He could look at her now; he saw surprise and almost fear written on her face. A light seemed to break through his brain; he knelt down beside her chair and took her hands; there was a curious break in his voice as he said : "I've come to tell you that I am free to marry you, Alida."

This book is full of love-making. Love-making is so easy to imagine up to a certain point. I can tell you what Jones said to Miss Smith ; what Jack said to Jill ; but I cannot tell you what Philip and Alida said to each other, because I do not know.

The clock striking five awoke Alida to a sense of her duties as a hostess.

"Why, you haven't had that tea you came for, yet," she said. "I must make it. Dorothy will be coming along in a minute, and she always clamors for something to eat."

They both laughed merrily at the remembrance of Philip's odd entrance, and Philip watched Alida setting the little table, and delayed rather than helped her with his masculine suggestions. In fact, the preparations would never have been complete had not Dorothy and Mr. Ashley arrived. Their arrival was not a noticeable fact, because where one went the other usually arrived; but on this occasion they came together, and there was about the two an air of submission and meekness that suggested that something had happened. While Dorothy was taking off her pretty wrap, she whispered to Alida in a despairing tone :

"It's all over ; we're engaged."

Alida wanted to laugh, but she sympathetically patted her friend's broad shoulder.

"I'm so glad, dear," she said. "Was your mother much upset?"

"Upset ! no," in the utmost exasperation. "No ; it's perfectly disheartening. It seems she wanted us to marry all along. Did you ever know anything so commonplace? I hoped at least she'd refuse her consent."

Since the musicale at Mrs. Beckington's when Philip suddenly became Jim's confidant, matters had been carried by her lover with a high hand. Dorothy was labelled "engaged" at last, and bore her new honors with much wailing to her intimates, and a great show of dignity to the outside world. Some water was needed for the tea, and Alida, kettle in hand, went into the kitchen to get it; and as a tea-kettle full of water is a heavy and unpleasant thing for a young lady to carry, of course Philip naturally followed her. Dorothy and Mr. Ashley were left alone for a moment in the studio. Dorothy heaved a deep, lugubrious sigh and sank sadly into a chair as far as possible from her *fiancé*.

"Everything is so dull and commonplace now, isn't it, Jim?"

Mr. Ashley laughed as he sat down on the arm of her chair and put his arm around her.

"Is everything so dull and commonplace now?"

"Yes; it isn't like the old times, when you used to have to snatch a kiss when no one was by."

"No one is by now," kissing her pink cheek.

"I hoped mother would refuse her consent, but you're so disgustingly eligible. Just think if you had been penniless or not in society, or anything terrible, and we should have had to elope!"

"But really, Dorothy, I don't

think your mother would have liked
you to elope."

" What a silly thing to say! " rising
with much scorn. " You haven't a
spark of romance in you."

" Very well, then ; I don't think
my mother would have liked me to
elope. Now, Dorothy, don't let's
quarrel. I'll be married in a balloon,
or up a tree, or anywhere that strikes
you as romantic ; I'm awfully sentimental about you."

The peal of the door-bell stopped
any further speech, Alida and Philip
coming back at the same time, as
though they had only taken the usual
time to fill the kettle. It was Mrs.
Beckington, utterly exhausted. She
sank into a chair by the door.

" Don't speak to me; and you
needn't shut the door—Clarence is
coming. Oh, I'm so tired ; I've got

the tea shakes. I've drank six cups
of tea. Tea! concoctions of everything in the world that is calculated
to shatter the nerves. Dorothy,
whatever form of enjoyment your
mother wishes to take for announcing
your engagement, don't let it be a
tea. I've been to three announcement teas this afternoon—such jams!
Really, I can't remember whether
Mabel Hawkins, in light blue, is going
to marry her cousin who is in the
army, or whether it is Louise Pome-
roy. Madame Calvé sang at the
Lawrence's, only their house was so
crowded you couldn't get near the
music room.''

Alida, all sympathy, flew to
Bertha's rescue; she took off her hat
and gave her a glass of sherry. Mrs.
Beckington suddenly caught sight of
her brother ; she was so tired that

she quite lost her head; no *ingénue*
could have been guilty of a more fearful remark than hers.

"Why, how did you come here,
Philip?" in a tone of the most
intense query and interest.

A dead silence followed. Mr.
Ashley alone, usually more remarkable for muscle than brains, came to
the rescue. He ignored her last
remark entirely.

"Yes, Mrs. Beckington, I entirely
agree with you ; Dorothy and I are
firm on one point : we won't have a
tea. Mrs. Mason may do her worst,
but I positively refuse to be the only
man in a tea fight, shaking hands and
having congratulations showered upon
me by thousands of women who don't
know me from Adam—or I them. I
hate tea—"

Dorothy's opinion of him rose as

he went on. She too would have liked to know why Philip was there, but she hadn't thought it good manners to ask when he was looking so absurdly happy. Luckily, before Jim's ideas and breath gave out, for the rest of the party seemed absolutely prostrated by Mrs. Beckington's extraordinary question, a welcome interruption came in the shape of Mr. Beckington and Gordon White.

"Heigho, Dorothy," was Mr. Beckington's cordial greeting, "I've just met your mother around at Tiffany's, ordering the cards for your announcement tea."

"Jim, be firm," said Dorothy, coming and standing beside her *fiancé*. "I won't marry you if we have to have it."

Jim felt that he must rise to the occasion; his recent success had elated him.

"If your mother insists upon it, I'll tell her I'll jilt you," he said with such earnestness that every one went off in shrieks of laughter.

It was the first time that Mr. White had been to Alida's studio. He thought it very charming; he looked around at the bits of color studies that she had up on the wall with the admiration of a connoisseur. Then there was the picture to be seen—the just-finished picture of "How Lisa Loved the King." They all grouped about it, the beautiful, richly colored picture into which Alida had worked so many of her cares and troubles, and which was finished. Finished ! Yes, as this chapter of her life is finished. To the others it was only a beautiful picture, but to Alida and Philip it was more ; and as her friends talked among themselves and admired all its beauties, Alida turned to Philip and looked at him with a glad light shining in her eyes; the light that told that she had indeed found her king.

And so we are going to leave Alida among her intimate friends and with her lover, for lovers and friends are a woman's life after all, however clever she may be with her brush or pen. Alida has lived thus far the life of a modern girl, in a position unique and peculiar to the nineteenth century; her future will lie in an entirely different one, which is neither unique nor peculiar to the nineteenth century, but which has been the highest sphere that a woman can hold since the world began, and will be until its end. She has served her apprenticeship nobly as a girl bachelor, and she will fill nobly the sacred position of wife and mother.

The years will go by; Dorothy and Jim will marry, Mr. Beckington will go on adoring his wife, who will for many years have a faithful devotee in Gordon White.

And what of Margaret? Word will come across the seas of the "American Duchess," for so she is called in love and honor by all who know her. She is noted far and wide for her goodness and charity, the light of her glorious charm and her devotion to her husband. She has reclaimed the name of her nation from that scorn of women who marry for position and title, and is happy as those are happy who live to be at peace with themselves, thankful that Providence in its mercy has allowed them to repair with their own hands the evil they have wrought.